AF241254

A KILLER IN THE KENNEL CLUB

Daring Dachshund Mystery, Book 2

By Cynthia Hickey

ISBN-13:978-1-968792-83-1

Chapter One

I couldn't find Bella. Fear skittered up my throat, and my heart lodged there right alongside it. Had she slipped out when I went to check the mail?

I opened the front door and called her name. Daisy kept yipping for me to retrieve her rubber, squeaky dachshund toy from under the couch, while Minnie barked at...nothing I could see. Another chaotic morning as the owner of three mini-dachshunds. "Bella!"

Tears burned my eyes as I called her name again, then darted around the common area of Riverside Towers. The morning air carried the faint smell of someone's coffee drifting from a cracked window above, and somewhere on the second floor, Mr. McIlroy's television droned through the wall. I glanced under every bush, peered behind the row of terra-cotta pots Mrs. Henderson kept lined up along the walkway like little clay soldiers, and even crouched to check beneath the wooden bench near the mailboxes. Nothing. Not a single low-slung, velvety body pressed flat against the concrete. Where could she be?

My chest tightened. Bella was the smallest of the three, at only eight pounds when she was soaking wet, and the most adventurous by a mile. Daisy caused trouble on purpose. Minnie caused it by accident. Bella caused it by sheer curiosity — nose to the ground, ears dragging, trotting after any scent that caught her attention without a single backward glance.

Fearing the worst, I returned to my apartment. "Bella!"

The front door swung shut behind me, and Daisy immediately abandoned her squeaky-toy campaign to run figure eights around my ankles. Minnie sat squarely in the middle of the rug, looking deeply offended by something only she could perceive. Neither of them offered any useful information. I checked behind the couch. Behind the armchair. Inside the bathroom. Empty.

I stepped into my bedroom with my heart in my throat, and there she was — her little chocolate-colored head barely visible above the mountain of bed pillows I'd stacked against the headboard, one dark eye blinking at me without so much as a flicker of guilt.

"You little scamp." Relief washed through me so fast it made me dizzy. I crossed the room, lifted her from her pillow fortress, and cradled her against my chest. She licked my chin exactly once — her version of a formal apology — then squirmed, which let me know that she considered the matter settled. I kissed her nose, breathed in the warm smell of her fur, and set her gently back among the pillows. She circled twice and collapsed like a deflating balloon.

Daisy chose that precise moment to renew her squeaky-toy emergency.

I could hear it from across the apartment. That desperate, repetitive yip that she reserved for genuine crises, which in Daisy's world meant the toy had traveled too far for her to reach it but not far enough for her to accept its loss. I found her still in the living room, front paws stretched flat under the sofa, nose nearly touching the baseboard, staring at the toy.

I lay prone on my belly and tried to reach it while all three dogs decided that this was the perfect moment to pile onto my head. Minnie stepped on my ear. Daisy abandoned the toy crisis to lick the back of my neck. Bella, who had apparently given up on her pillow sanctuary at the first sound of group activity, grabbed my ponytail in a vain attempt to drag me backward across the hardwood floor like a very small, very determined sled dog.

"Stop it, girls. You aren't making this any easier."

How in the world had the toy gotten so far under the sofa? I stretched until my shoulder ached, fingertips grazing it once, twice, before I finally got a grip. Three dachshunds cheered by climbing further onto my back.

Someone knocked on the door. "Come in!"

I used what little core strength I had left after three months of mostly gentle tenant-management duties to push myself upward. Success. I lifted the toy triumphantly into the air, then threw it the full length of the living room for Daisy to chase. She caught it mid-bounce, pranced back to the sofa, and, with an expression of utter satisfaction, shoved it firmly back underneath.

I straightened my ponytail and accepted my fate.

Linda Hooper, once a murder suspect, now my best friend, stepped through the door with the easy confidence of someone who had never once doubted her welcome. She wore a floral blouse tucked into wide-leg trousers and carried a reusable tote bag printed with cartoon dogs that I strongly suspected she had purchased specifically to impress my girls. It was working. Minnie sat down at her feet like a disciple.

"How soon you forget that killers walk among us." Linda draped herself against the doorframe before making her entrance properly. "Crystal Waters, I have the perfect way to relieve your boredom."

"The killer was three months ago." I pushed to my feet and straightened my ponytail a second time, since Bella had already begun working it loose again from her position on the arm of the sofa. "And I'm not bored."

I glanced at my dogs, who were currently

engaged in a rotating cycle of yipping, barking at the wall, and relocating the squeaky toy to an even more inaccessible position. Daisy paused long enough to give me a long, knowing look.

Well. Maybe a little.

With my boyfriend, Lance, back full-time with the Riverside PD, his schedule had returned to its usual rhythm of unpredictable shifts and late nights, which meant our quiet evenings together had become rarer. And with a maintenance crew now hired to handle the yard work — a concession I'd made after the great hedge-trimming incident of September — my days had narrowed down to dogs, bills, the occasional tenant complaint, and approximately forty-five minutes of daily reading that I kept falling asleep during. I loved my life. I genuinely did. But love didn't always mean thrilling.

"What's your grand idea?"

Linda's grin spread wide and satisfied as she settled onto the sofa, accepted Minnie onto her lap, and scratched Bella under the chin with the practiced ease of someone who knew exactly how much pressure to use and where.

"The Riverside Kennel Club."

I blinked. "Dog politics? No, thanks."

"It is not politics." She gave me a look of patient but firm correction. "It's war with paws and bows. Which, I grant you, is more entertaining than politics by a significant margin." She nodded toward my three.

"Your girls would do well. They're beautiful, they're spirited, and they have personality to spare. As a professional dog walker, I have seen what wins ribbons and what just takes up space in the ring, and these three have what it takes." She paused for effect. "Also, Daisy has a naturally competitive spirit. You can see it in the way she eyes other dogs on the street."

This was unfortunately accurate. Daisy had opinions about other dogs that she expressed freely and at volume.

"I volunteer at the club," Linda continued, apparently reading my hesitation as the beginning of a cave rather than a refusal. "I can introduce you to everyone who matters. And before you say anything about the time commitment, it's one meeting. Tomorrow night at the Riverside Community Center. Six o'clock." She stood, returning Minnie gently to the floor, where she immediately went to bark at the door. "I'll pick you up at five-thirty. You can bring these three."

"What's on your agenda today?" she asked brightly, already moving toward the door.

I sighed and counted on my fingers. "A light is out in the laundromat. One of the washing machines is off-balance and sounds like it's trying to walk across the floor with every spin cycle. Mrs. Henderson says there's a bad smell coming from under her kitchen sink, and I'm half-convinced it's the drain gasket, but it could be worse." I paused. "Oh, and someone on the third floor submitted a written complaint about the parking lot lighting, which I agree with but haven't budgeted for yet."

Linda tilted her head with the expression of someone who had just proven their point for them. "And then what?"

I opened my mouth. Closed it.

She smiled with enormous kindness. "It'll be fun, Crystal. I promise. These girls need an outlet for all that..." she gestured at the living room, where Daisy had resumed her squeaky-toy campaign, Minnie had shifted from barking at the door to barking at me, and Bella was attempting to open the kitchen cabinet where the treats were kept by pawing at it with both front feet and determination. "...energy."

With her smile still fully in place, she sashayed out of my apartment, the door clicking shut behind her, apparently not taking no for an answer and not concerned that I hadn't given her a yes either. That was Linda. She operated on the assumption that people would eventually arrive at the right conclusion, and that the right conclusion was always hers.

I stood in the middle of my living room for a moment, listening to the morning sounds of Riverside Towers. The distant rumble of the faulty washing machine that I really did need to fix today, the murmur of televisions and voices filtering through walls, the scratch of Bella's small paw against the cabinet door.

"You three try to behave." I reached for my tool

belt from the hook by the door. I buckled it on with the familiar weight of purpose that came with having something useful to do. "I'll take you for a walk when I get back."

Daisy squeaked the toy once in acknowledgment. Minnie barked at the radiator. Bella looked up from the cabinet, considered me for a moment with those deep, liquid eyes, and then went back to the project at hand.

I grabbed my key ring and headed out into the hallway, already mentally sorting the order of repairs. Light bulb in the laundromat first. Then the washing machine. Then Mrs. Henderson's sink, which I suspected would take the longest and smell the worst.

And somewhere in the back of my mind, quiet and persistent as Bella at a cabinet door, was the image of three dachshunds, one smooth-haired and two long-haired, trotting around a show ring — ears flying, tails up — causing absolute havoc among the dog-bow-and-politics crowd of the Riverside Kennel Club.

Maybe Linda wasn't entirely wrong.

Not that I was going to tell her that until at least five-thirty tomorrow.

Chapter Two

I stood at the front of the line at the Riverside Kennel Club meeting and glared at the woman behind the sign-in desk. "Minnie is not fat."

I glanced at her name tag. Vivian Cargill. The name suited her somehow. Sharp and a little pinched, like her features.

The woman peered at me over the rim of her glasses. "She weighs 13.5 pounds. To qualify as a miniature, she cannot exceed 12 pounds, and she doesn't weigh enough to be a standard. Her ears are also too short." She set down her pen. "She may be a purebred, but she isn't perfect. You still qualify to become a member, if you wish, because the other two meet all of the criteria." Her gaze dropped to the paper in front of her. "Especially Clarabella. Bella, as you call her."

She glanced past me to where Bella and Daisy had already managed to wind their leashes into a configuration that defied basic geometry. A muscle twitched near her mouth. Not quite a smile and not quite a grimace. Something precise and unpleasant that lived exactly between the two.

"We will be cleaning house soon, Miss Waters. Do keep that in mind. All animals must be well-trained and obedient."

Minnie, as if she understood every word and had decided to make my evening as difficult as possible, chose this moment to plant her haunches on the floor and stare at Vivian with the brand of dachshund stubbornness that I had long since stopped trying to argue with.

"Don't worry." A woman with a sleek, copper-coated Doberman strolled past the desk without breaking stride. "She's a cold-blooded…"She said the last word quietly but clearly, and it was not a nice one.

Vivian's expression didn't flicker. Apparently, she'd heard it before.

"Come on, Crystal." Linda appeared at my elbow and steered me away from the desk, the way you'd redirect someone from an argument they couldn't win in a room full of witnesses. "Let's get some snacks before the meeting starts. I'll introduce you to the people who actually matter."

I glanced back at Vivian, who had already moved on to scrutinizing the next arrival with her clipboard. "I'm not sure I'm interested in joining a club if everyone is like her."

"Don't mind her." Linda kept walking. "She had

to buy a papered Pomeranian just to get in because her previous dog had a significant underbite. She's been overcompensating ever since." She shot the woman a grin over her shoulder that Vivian either didn't see or chose to ignore. "The Pomeranian hasn't won a thing. She blames everyone but herself."

We reached a long table spread with finger foods. Small sandwiches, cheese arranged in careful rows, something wrapped in prosciutto that Bella immediately stretched toward on her hind legs. I redirected her with a gentle tug and loaded a small plate.

"All right." I scanned the room over the rim of my plate. "Who's who?"

Linda turned beside me and surveyed the crowd. The community center had filled up more than I'd expected. Dogs of every size milled between their owners' legs. Some sitting with rigid show-ring composure, others less disciplined, noses working the air near the food table with interest.

"The woman with the Doberman is Angela Merritt. The dog is Sweetie Pie, which is the single most misleading name in this room. She's won more awards than anyone here, and Angela knows it, and Vivian *really* knows it." She nodded toward a compact woman in a cream blazer who stood near the center of the room with the ease of someone entirely accustomed to being looked at. "That argument you saw at the desk is a recurring event. Different words, same outcome."

Angela caught my eye briefly, assessed me with the quick efficiency of someone who made evaluations for sport, and returned her attention to the woman she'd been speaking with.

"The one she's talking to is Geraldine Walsh. Everyone calls her Gerry. She's the club president and breeds Yorkies. She's the reason this group functions at all. Without her, Vivian would have run off half the members by now." Linda pointed subtly toward a shorter woman near the far end of the food table who fussed over the arrangement of what appeared to be homemade pastries. "That's Patricia Donnelly — Trish. She made most of what's on this table. She owns two French Bulldogs, and she is, without question, the best baker in town. Do not leave without trying the lemon shortbread." She paused. "And the man near the door, tall, dark jacket, that's Colin Hart. He's a professional handler and organizes the yearly dog show. If you ever decide to compete, he's the person worth knowing."

I glanced toward Angela and Vivian, who had resumed what appeared to be a pointed exchange near the sign-in table. "Those two seem like they've been at it for a while."

"Years," Linda said simply. "Vivian spent three thousand dollars on that Pomeranian, and she has not placed in a single competition. Angela wins consistently, makes it look effortless, and doesn't bother to pretend she isn't aware of the gap." She sipped from her cup. "Vivian takes snarky comments seriously.

Angela takes winning seriously. They're never going to like each other."

Before I could respond, Minnie stiffened beside me and let out a low, grumbling growl. I looked down. Vivian had materialized from somewhere to my left, the two Pomeranians, Honey and Sugar, if their matching collars were any indication, trotted at her heels like small, opinionated clouds. They eyed Minnie with the haughty disinterest of dogs who had been extensively informed of their own importance.

Vivian's expression as she passed was the specific look of someone filing away evidence. "Well-behaved, Miss Waters. I do hope you'll keep that in mind going forward."

"She's only growling, Vivian." I stressed her first name with what I hoped was pleasant deliberateness. "Why don't you call me Crystal, since I'll be a member?" I heard myself say it before I'd fully made the decision and was mildly surprised to find I meant it.

The look on Vivian's face suggested the same surprise, and considerably less pleasure.

"Glad to hear it." A warm voice cut in from my right, and a plump woman with silver-streaked hair and the easy smile of someone who had been defusing moments like this one for years appeared beside me. She extended her hand. "Gerry Walsh. Club president. And what gorgeous dachshunds you have."

I tossed Vivian a look over Gerry's shoulder that I'm not particularly proud of. "Thank you very much."

"Again, Gerry." Vivian's voice had taken on the strained patience of a woman who felt her objections were being ignored, which they were. "I do think the club's reputation would benefit from a focus on more refined breeds."

"Such as?" Gerry tilted her head with the pleasant openness of someone who already knew the answer and wanted to hear it said aloud in front of witnesses.

Vivian didn't answer that directly.

"All of our requirements state that animals must be purebred," Gerry continued. "These three meet that criteria. I've reviewed their paperwork personally, and they are not pet-class animals, regardless of what anyone might prefer to assume." She rested a hand briefly on Vivian's shoulder. "Come sit in the front row. We're nearly ready to start. The competition discussion alone will take us forty minutes."

Vivian went. She didn't look happy about it, but she went.

"What does pet-class mean?" I asked once both women had moved out of earshot.

"That they're not show dogs." Linda steered us toward the rows of folding chairs filling the center of the room. "Quality animals, just not competing stock. Vivian would love to use it as a polite way to say your girls don't belong here. Gerry won't allow it."

"Back row, please." I wasn't ready to be seen clearly by anyone with a clipboard.

We found two chairs at the far end of the last row, and I looped all three leashes around my wrist and took stock of where I was.

The community center smelled like coffee and dog and the lavender hand lotion of whoever sat in front of us. Around the room, people settled into seats while dogs arranged themselves with varying degrees of cooperation beneath chairs and across laps.

Colin Hart stood near the front, talking quietly with a man I didn't recognize. Angela Merritt sat in the third row with Sweetie Pie lying at her feet like a copper statue, still as a show dog, which she presumably was.

"I've never thought about competing before," I said.

"Bella would be perfect if she cooperates." Linda reached down and scratched my smallest behind one ear. Bella leaned into it briefly, then went back to watching the room with an alert focus. "She's a bit skittish, though. The ring might be too much for her. And she still hates the leash, doesn't she."

"Sometimes she walks," I said. "Sometimes she sits down and becomes a small, furry anchor."

"It's the harness she hates," Linda said. "You can see it the moment you pick it up. She reads your intention before you've even moved."

"She's only timid until she sees a squirrel," I said. "Or a rabbit. Or a longhorn cow, which is a long story involving a farm visit I will not be repeating. The moment she spots something she's decided is prey, she forgets she weighs eight pounds and acts like she can take on anything breathing."

Linda laughed, quietly enough not to draw attention. Daisy took the opportunity to nose my jacket pocket in search of treats, found none, and expressed her feelings about this by stepping firmly on my foot and sitting down on it.

Minnie had stopped growling. She sat upright between my ankles with her ears swiveled toward the front of the room, as Gerry took her place behind the podium.

I looped the leashes a little tighter around my wrist and settled back in my chair.

Whatever the Riverside Kennel Club turned out to be, it was already more complicated than a hobby. There was Vivian's clipboard and her three-thousand-dollar grievance. There was Angela Merritt and what she'd said as she walked past the desk. There was Colin Hart and his yearly dog show, and the quiet power that came with being the person who decided what won.

And there was Bella, eight pounds of selective courage, sitting pressed against my ankle, watching everything.

Maybe Linda wasn't wrong after all.

Chapter Three

I watched as Angela put Sweetie Pie through her paces along the open stretch of floor Colin had cleared at the front of the room. The Doberman moved with a fluid, unhurried precision that was genuinely impressive. Head up, gait even, each step placed with the confidence of a dog who had done this ten thousand times and found it mildly beneath her.

My dogs could totally do that. As long as there were no distractions, no enticing aroma of treats, no sudden movement in the periphery, and absolutely no rabbit, squirrel, or longhorn cow within a quarter mile.

I kept that thought to myself.

Beside me, Linda had gone still in the way she did when something worth watching was happening. Bella had leaned up on, wanting to be in my lap. I picked her up and she started monitoring the room with the low, quiet alertness she reserved for situations she hadn't yet decided how to feel about. Daisy sat upright on my other side, ears forward. Minnie had fallen asleep sometime during the treasurer's report and was now a warm, snoring weight across the top of my foot.

"She should hold her head higher." Vivian's voice came from two rows ahead of us, from where she stood against the wall, aimed toward the front of the room without quite being loud enough to be considered an outright interruption. Just loud enough to be heard. "Your dog is slipping."

The room went still.

Angela stopped. Sweetie Pie stopped with her, reading her handler the way good dogs do, one ear rotating back. Angela turned to face Vivian with the measured, controlled movement of a woman deciding how much of herself to expend on this. "She is showing a perfect example of how a dog should perform in the show ring."

"Not by my calculations."

"You don't own this club." A slow flush rose in Angela's face. "And your calculations haven't won you a ribbon in two years, so I'd think carefully about offering them."

"I wish I had some popcorn," Linda whispered beside me. "This is genuinely some show."

"It really does look as if she hates her." I kept my voice low and put a steadying hand on Bella, who had begun to tremble. She wasn't the only one. Around the room, other dogs had picked up on something in the air and had pressed closer to their owners. Even Sweetie Pie had shifted her weight, her attention moving between Angela and Vivian with the wariness of a dog who had seen this before and knew how it ended.

"They do hate each other," Linda said. "Two years running. It started when Sweetie Pie beat Honey in the spring regional. Vivian never forgave Angela for winning, and she never forgave the judges for allowing it."

"You're going to be the first person booted from this club!" Vivian's voice had climbed past its earlier precision into something unsteady. She gathered herself with visible effort, smoothed the front of her jacket, and stormed back to her seat with Honey and Sugar trotting at her heels.

Angela watched her go. "You have no grounds." Her voice had dropped, which somehow made it carry further than the shouting had. "My dog is the best one in this room, her bloodline is without question, and every judge in the regional circuit knows both of those things."

"All right, ladies." Gerry Walsh got to her feet. "Have a seat, Angela. We'll move on to the next item on the agenda. There's no need for tempers to flare." She glanced toward the back of the room and sent a warm, apologetic smile in my direction. "We do have a new prospective member with us this evening."

Angela sat. Vivian stared at the front wall. Between them, the room exhaled.

Minnie slept through all of it.

The meeting continued. Gerry steered it with the

efficiency of someone who had long ago learned to keep things moving as the surest defense against further eruptions. The upcoming regional competition. Entry deadlines. A discussion about the new scoring criteria that went on longer than necessary but produced no additional drama. Trish Donnelly raised a point about the awards banquet venue that everyone seemed to have an opinion on but no one seemed willing to decide. Colin Hart said very little but listened in the attentive way of someone keeping score.

Halfway through, with the agenda apparently stable and Linda perfectly capable of managing three dachshunds for five minutes, I excused myself quietly and slipped out through the side door toward the hallway.

The restroom was at the far end, past the bulletin board plastered with flyers for obedience classes and a faded notice about a lost Cavalier King Charles from eight months ago. I pushed inside, relieved to find it empty, and took the far stall.

Less than a minute passed before the door opened.

I recognized the voices immediately. Angela and Vivian, apparently not finished, and unaware or unconcerned that they'd followed each other into a restroom to continue what the meeting room had interrupted. There was a specific kind of anger that didn't care about venue. This was it.

They weren't talking about dogs this time.

The shift was subtle but distinct. The vocabulary

was the same, the heat was the same, but the shape of what they were saying had changed. Less about ribbons and bloodlines and more about something else entirely, something with edges I couldn't quite make out from behind a closed stall door.

"You can't prove anything." Angela's voice had gone flat and controlled. Whatever Vivian had said or implied, Angela wasn't rattled by it.

"Oh, I can." Vivian's said. "And I will."

Footsteps crossed the tile. The door opened and swung shut, hard.

I stayed where I was.

Silence settled in. The kind that follows an exit and waits to see whether it sticks. Then the sound of a faucet running. One person was still in the room. I tracked the sound without moving: the water, the pump of the soap dispenser, the water again, the mechanical grind of the paper towel dispenser.

I had no reason to keep still. I was in a restroom stall, and the meeting was waiting, and I had three dachshunds in Linda's capable but finite patience. I had every reasonable justification for opening the door, washing my hands, and walking back out.

And yet.

The door opened again. Different footsteps this time — lighter, quicker, less certain. Someone who had come in and then thought better of announcing themselves. A pause. Then a voice, low enough that the words dissolved before they reached me, leaving only tone behind. The tone was not friendly.

I didn't move. Bella would have called it good instinct. I called it the stillness that comes from standing very quietly in a situation that has stopped feeling ordinary.

Then a loud thud. Something solid and heavy. Not a fist against a wall, not a door thrown open, but something with weight behind it, a sound that landed wrong in a room that had been quiet a second before.

The door opened. The door closed.

I stood in the stall and counted to ten. Then I counted to ten again. I wasn't sure why the reluctance to step from the stall, but instinct…maybe a trickle of fear…kept me inside.

The restroom was silent. Not the comfortable silence of an empty room either.

I waited to see whether anyone else would come in. Nobody did.

Whatever had just happened in thirty square feet of community center restroom, it had resolved itself, or at least gone somewhere else. The faucet wasn't running. No footsteps, no voices, no movement I could detect. Just the faint hum of the ventilation overhead and the distant, muffled rhythm of Gerry's voice resuming the meeting on the other side of the wall.

My hand rested against the stall door. I hadn't noticed putting it there.

I thought about Angela's voice with that careful flatness when she said *you can't prove anything.* The phrasing of someone who had already considered what there was to prove and had built a position around it. I thought about Vivian's answer, which wasn't a denial. It was a promise. *I can. And I will.* Two sentences, both short, and both pointing in the same direction.

I thought about the thud.

The sensible thing, the practical, uncomplicated thing, was to open the door, wash my hands, and go back to my seat where my dogs waited, and the meeting was still ongoing, and nothing had technically happened that I could point to and name.

I was the property manager of Riverside Towers. I had a washing machine to fix tomorrow morning, a light bulb in the laundromat, and Mrs. Henderson's kitchen sink still unresolved. I had three dachshunds who needed a walk, a boyfriend who was working a late shift, not to mention a very reasonable life that did not require me to stand motionless in a restroom stall because two women had argued in front of me and one of them had made a sound I didn't like.

I thought about what Linda had said this morning as she leaned against my doorframe with that wide, certain smile.

How soon you forget that killers walk among us.

I reached for the latch.

Chapter Four

I rushed from the stall, slipped, stumbled, and went down hard on both knees. My first thought was purely that someone needed to put up a wet floor sign, because this kind of standing water was a liability. My second thought arrived a half-second later and erased the first entirely.

I stared into the dead, sightless eyes of Vivian Cargill.

I hadn't slipped in water. Blood pooled dark and wide beneath her head, spreading across the grout lines in the tile. A knife — handle up, blade buried — jutted from her chest. My palms were on the floor. I looked at them. Blood. I looked at my knees. More blood, soaked through the fabric of my pants in two wide, dark patches.

I scrambled backward until my shoulders hit the stall door and I screamed.

Within seconds, the restroom filled with people. The noise from the meeting room spilled in with them.

Chairs scraping, voices overlapping, and then it went oddly quiet as those in the room processed what they were looking at.

Angela went white before she pushed past two people without a word and made it into the nearest stall. A second later came the unmistakable sound of violent vomiting.

"Oh, this is not going to be good for the club's reputation." Trish pressed one hand over her mouth. Her eyes were wide above her fingers, moving between the body and the blood on my clothes.

"What a thing to say." Gerry Walsh's voice came out sharp and steady, the voice she used to cut off arguments in the meeting room, and it worked here too. "Someone call 911. Colin —" She turned to where Hart stood in the doorway, one hand braced against the frame. "Get these people out. All of them. Right now."

He moved. To his credit, he didn't ask questions; he just started turning people back through the door with the quiet efficiency of a man useful in a crisis. Most of them went without much resistance. Horror had a way of making people cooperative.

Linda appeared at the edge of the crowd, all three dachshunds somehow compressed into her arms in a configuration that suggested at least two of them were sharing the same space. She took one look at me on the floor, one look at Vivian, said "Oh," in a very small voice, and backed out. She returned thirty seconds later without the dogs. "Don't worry. They're tied to a chair."

From the other side of the door came the distinctive sound of a chair being dragged across a tiled floor, accompanied by what I recognized as Daisy's particular pitch of indignation.

I was still on the floor. I hadn't fully registered that yet. The tile felt cold through my pants, and my hands were shaking. Then my gaze went to the counter.

The marble soap dispenser, the heavy, rounded one that should have been sitting beside the faucet, was on the floor under the sink, pushed back against the cabinet face. Blood covered the corner of it in a dark, deliberate smear that didn't look like a splash or a spatter. It looked like contact.

I looked back at the knife.

The knife was wrong. Not wrong in the obvious way, though it was obviously, terribly wrong, but wrong in a way that I couldn't quite articulate from the floor with blood on my hands. Why use the dispenser and then the knife? One or the other suggested intent. Both suggested something else, something more complicated and less clean, and whatever that was, it sat in the back of my mind like a splinter I couldn't reach.

I pressed my back against the wall and used it to push myself upright. My knees protested. My whole body felt like it had been rearranged slightly from the inside.

"Are you all right?" Linda skirted around the blood with the careful sidestep of someone navigating a crime scene for the second time in recent memory and came to stand beside me. "Who did this?"

"I didn't see." I meant it, and I also meant the other thing behind it — that I had heard something, and that what I'd heard was going to matter, and that the right person to hear it first was not anyone currently standing in this bathroom. I kept my mouth shut.

Gerry wet some paper towels and then pressed them into my hands. "Try to clean yourself up, dear. The police will be here soon." She glanced toward the stall where the sound of vomiting had subsided into silence. "Angela. When you're able, please fetch Crystal a chair."

The chair appeared a few minutes later, carried out by Angela, who had regained approximately half her color and all of her composure. She set it down without meeting my eyes and went to stand near the door with her arms crossed. Had she figured out I'd been in the stall during her argument with Vivan?

I sat. I cleaned my hands as well as paper towels allowed, which was not well at all. I stared at the floor and waited.

Lance arrived fifteen minutes later. He came through the door in his jacket, badge already out, and took in the room in the methodical way he had — not fast, not slow, just thorough, moving from the body to the dispenser to me in a sequence that I recognized as a professional assessment being performed with some effort to suppress personal alarm.

He looked at Linda. He looked at Gerry. He looked at Angela, who still faced the door.

"Out. All three of you. Nobody leaves the building. I mean no one leaves this facility." He waited while they moved, Linda giving my arm a brief, firm squeeze as she passed. Once the door closed, his gaze came to rest on me with an entirely different quality. "You okay? Are you hurt?"

"I'm fine." The tears arrived.

"Can you tell me what happened?" He crouched to look at the knee prints in the blood and didn't comment on them directly. "You stumbled across the body."

"I did. I was in the last stall." I dropped the ruined paper towels in the trash. "I heard Vivian and Angela arguing."

"Last names." He straightened. The shift was instantaneous from concerned to professional, boyfriend to detective, the seam between them barely visible.

"Vivian Cargill and Angela Merritt. I just met them tonight, so —" I pressed my fingers to my forehead briefly. "Angela said Vivian couldn't prove anything. Vivian said she could and would. Then someone left. Someone else came in, not Vivian — she must have already been on the floor by then, or —" I stopped and took a deep breath. "The second person who came in said something too quietly for me to make out. Then there was a thud. I stayed in the stall until everything went quiet."

"Why didn't you come out when you heard the thud?"

I frowned at him. "Because I didn't want whoever had just made that sound to know I was there. They'd already killed one person."

He accepted this without argument, which told me he thought it was reasonable, which did not make me feel particularly better. "Did you touch anything?"

"No. Just the floor when I fell. I may have touched her when I went down." I swallowed. "Lance. The knife isn't what killed her. Look at the soap dispenser under the counter. The blood on it…it's the corner. Someone hit her with it first. The knife came after."

He looked at the dispenser without moving toward it. His expression didn't change, but something behind his eyes did. "I see it."

He was quiet for a moment. Around us, the restroom was very still, the fluorescent bulb still flickering above the second sink, Vivian still on the floor with the knife still wrong in the middle of everything.

"Crystal." He took me by the arm, gently and with more care than the detective voice would have suggested. "Go home. I'll come by later for a full statement. Get Linda to drive you." He paused. "I'll have someone bring your car."

"I came with Linda."

He nodded. "I have to admit, a kennel club wasn't what I expected when Linda called this in."

"I wasn't expecting it either." I took a breath that came out less steady than I'd intended. "Vivian made a comment about Minnie's weight at the sign-in desk. I joined out of spite."

It was such a small, ridiculous reason, and the tears that came with it were out of proportion to everything except the fact that I was standing in a bathroom with blood on my knees and a dead woman on the floor, and I had walked into this evening because of a comment about a dog's weight.

Lance looked at me for a moment with something that wasn't quite a smile but wasn't far from one either. He led me out by the arm and transferred me to Linda. "I'll be by later to speak with both of you."

"Understood." Linda got a hand under my elbow and navigated me past the cluster of people still waiting in the hall under the watchful eye of a uniformed officer, past Colin Hart sitting very still in a folding chair near the entrance, past Gerry speaking quietly into her phone, and out through the double doors into the cool evening air.

The dachshunds were in the back seat. Minnie was asleep. Daisy had the squeaky toy, which I had no memory of anyone bringing, and was working it steadily. Bella pressed her nose to my neck the moment I sat down and stayed there, warm and certain, all the way home.

The drive was quiet. Linda shot me glances at the traffic lights but didn't ask anything. She had always known when to wait.

"Why did no one seem shocked?" I said finally, as she turned into the Riverside Towers lot. "Angela was sick, but after that, no one seemed surprised. No one seemed to even care."

Linda pulled into a space and cut the engine. "Vivian wasn't well liked."

I watched the parking lot lights reflect off the windshield. Minnie snored. "That's not a reason to be cold about a murder. She was difficult, but she didn't deserve to be beaten to death on a bathroom floor."

Linda didn't answer right away. "No," she said at last. "She didn't."

We sat there a moment longer than we needed to, the car ticking as the engine cooled, the night outside ordinary and indifferent to everything that had happened in the last hour. Then Linda opened her door, and I opened mine, and we got the dogs inside and turned on all the lights, because some evenings you just need the lights on.

Chapter Five

Lance let himself in a little after eight with his own key, which still gave me a small, warm feeling I hadn't entirely gotten used to. I heard the lock turn and didn't move from the sofa, mostly because moving would have required negotiating with three dachshunds who had arranged themselves across me and considered the afghan communal property and my presence beneath it a courtesy they were extending.

Bella was tucked under my chin. Minnie had claimed my feet. Daisy was somewhere in the middle, her spine pressed against my stomach, the squeaky toy wedged between us like a chaperone.

He came in, took one look at the arrangement, and didn't say anything about it. That was one of the things I liked about him. He'd learned early that commenting on the dogs' furniture habits was a debate he wasn't going to win. I'd seen his German Shepherd, King, on his sofa a time or two.

He shrugged off his jacket, disappeared into the

kitchen, and came back with two glasses of wine. He set both on the coffee table, then sat beside me, lifted my legs, and settled them across his lap. He handed me a glass. He rubbed my feet through the afghan with one hand, which caused Minnie to relocate to the back of the sofa with the affronted dignity of someone who'd had their armchair taken.

We sat like that for a minute without talking. The apartment was quiet — not peaceful exactly, but settled, like water that's stopped moving. Outside, someone in the parking lot had their radio on, just barely audible through the window.

"I'm sorry if I seemed brusque today." He kept his eyes on his glass. "It's not a simple line to walk. Keeping the job separate from everything else."

"I know." I meant it. "You were professional. That's what the situation needed."

He nodded once, accepting that without making more of it.

"We took Angela in for questioning."

I sat up. Bella made a sound of protest and relocated to my lap in a tighter, more pointed arrangement. "I don't think she did it."

He looked at me with the expression that meant he was listening in the professional sense. Not agreeing or dismissing, just opening a door and waiting to see what came through it. "What makes you say that?"

"The timing doesn't hold up." I tucked my feet more firmly under his hand, partly for warmth and partly because it helped me think. "They went into the restroom together. If Angela wanted Vivian dead, she had her alone in a small room with a marble soap dispenser and a knife . Which means someone brought a knife, which means this wasn't impulsive. So why leave? Why have the argument, leave, and then come back? If she came back to finish it, why whisper? You don't whisper to a woman you're about to kill. You'd just do it."

Lance was quiet for a moment. "You worked that out quickly."

"I had a long drive home and three dogs who weren't talking. Plus, Linda seemed to sense I wasn't in a talking mood." I sipped my wine. "Too many pieces that don't fit Angela. She's angry, and she's blunt, and she hates Vivian openly, in front of witnesses, all evening. That's not how someone behaves when they're planning to kill a person in the next twenty minutes."

He didn't confirm or deny any of it, which was its own kind of answer. "She says she didn't do it. That after she left the restroom the first time, she went back to the meeting room, and she didn't see Vivian again until she entered with the rest of the crowd."

"Did anyone see her? In the meeting room, I mean. Between the time she left the restroom and the time things went loud."

"We're looking into that."

I recognized the phrasing. It meant yes, they were, and no, he wasn't going to tell me what they'd found. I let it sit. "What did she say when she found out I'd been in the stall the whole time?"

Something shifted in his expression, subtle enough that I might have missed it if I hadn't been watching. "She seemed surprised."

"Surprised how?"

"The kind of surprised that isn't entirely comfortable." He set his glass on the coffee table. "She recovered quickly. But there was a moment."

I thought about that. Angela, in the restroom doorway with the chair, not meeting my eyes. Angela standing with her arms crossed, facing away from Vivian. The word *surprised* was doing a lot of work in that sentence.

If Angela hadn't killed Vivian, she still knew something. Or suspected something. Or had heard something in that restroom that she hadn't shared with the police yet and wasn't sure whether to. The surprise at finding out I'd been present the whole time was like that of someone who'd been reconstructing a sequence of events and had just discovered a piece they hadn't accounted for.

Which meant the same thing it had meant in the car on the way home, when I'd first thought it and then let the wine, the dogs, and the afghan push it aside temporarily.

Whoever had whispered. Whoever had made the thud. That person had no reason to believe there'd been a witness. And now, thanks to Lance's interview with

Angela, they might.

"Lance." I put my glass down. "If Angela didn't already know someone else was in that restroom, and now she does —"

"I know." He said it quietly and without hesitation, which meant he'd already been there. He'd arrived at this apartment, poured two glasses of wine, and rubbed my feet, with this already sitting in the back of his mind. "We were careful about what we shared with her. But I can't guarantee what gets said in a building full of people who were all interviewed tonight." He looked at me directly. "You need to be careful, Crystal."

"I didn't see anything."

"You heard something."

"I heard two women arguing, a door, some footsteps, and a thud. I can't identify any voice except Vivian's and Angela's, and only because I'd been listening to them argue all evening. I don't know whether the second person is male or female." I picked up my glass again, mostly to have something to do with my hands. "I'm not a threat to anyone."

"You don't know that, and neither do I, and neither does whoever was in that bathroom."

The wine was good. I focused on that for a moment — the dry, clean taste of it, the way it was an ordinary thing in an evening that had stopped being ordinary several hours ago. Bella shifted in my lap and rested her chin on my knee, her eyes moving between

Lance and me with the watchful attention she gave to conversations she'd decided were significant.

"Tell me about the knife," I said.

He looked at me.

"You know I'm going to think about this regardless. Tell me something useful, and I'll think about it more productively."

He was quiet for long enough that I thought he was going to decline. Then: "It wasn't from the community center kitchen. The style is wrong It isn't a catering knife, or a utility knife. Someone brought it specifically."

"So premeditated."

"On someone's part. Whether that's the person who used it or whether someone else brought it, and the opportunity presented itself —" He shook his head slightly. "We don't know yet."

I thought about the soap dispenser again. The blood on the corner of it. Vivian hit from behind, or from the side, already going down. Then the knife, after. Two weapons, two different kinds of violence. One was impulsive, and one had been carried into the building in someone's bag or coat pocket. It was the combination that nagged at me. Either the knife was always the plan, and the dispenser was opportunistic, or the dispenser was the actual weapon, and the knife was something else entirely, like staging, insurance, or an attempt to complicate the picture.

Or two different people, which opened a door I

wasn't ready to walk through yet.

"What was Vivian saying she could prove?" I asked.

Lance looked at me again with that same careful assessment. "What makes you think it was about something provable?"

"The way she said it. It wasn't *I'll tell everyone* or *I'll ruin you.* She said *I can and I will,* which implies evidence. Documentation. Something concrete." I scratched Bella's ear absently. "Vivian had something. A photograph, records, something she'd been holding and decided tonight was the night to use it."

"Or she thought she had something," Lance said carefully, "and whoever she said it to disagreed."

That landed differently. Not a secret being suppressed. A claim being disputed. Someone who believed Vivian was wrong, or bluffing, or that whatever she had could be explained away or taken back. And if Vivian had it on her, in a purse, in a phone, then the restroom was also a retrieval, not just a silencing.

Daisy squeaked the toy.

The sound was so abrupt and so thoroughly out of keeping with everything that both Lance and I startled, and then he let out a short, tired laugh that I was glad to hear.

"She's been doing that at irregular intervals all evening," I said. "I think she's processing."

"Smart dog." He reached over and scratched

Daisy's ears, which she accepted as her due. His hand stayed there for a moment before dropping back to my ankle. "I need you to stay out of this, Crystal."

"I'm already in it. I have Vivian's blood on a pair of pants that I'm fairly certain are ruined."

"You know what I mean."

I did. And I understood why he was asking, and I understood the difference between understanding something and agreeing to it. I thought Lance probably understood that too, which was why he was looking at me with an expression somewhere between trust and resignation, with a layer of genuine worry underneath both.

"I'll be careful." Which was true.

He seemed to recognize it for what it was. He squeezed my ankle once, picked up his glass, and leaned back into the sofa cushions with the slow exhale of a man who had done what he could for the evening.

Minnie climbed back down from the sofa arm, circled twice, and settled against his hip like she'd decided the dispute over foot space was resolved.

Outside, the radio in the parking lot had gone quiet.

Chapter Six

The Riverside Kennel Club held its weekly volunteer morning on Thursdays, which Linda had failed to mention when she'd handed me a membership form and a schedule with the cheerful attitude of someone who had already decided how my Thursdays were going to go.

I showed up at nine with Bella, Daisy, and Minnie because Linda had assured me dogs were welcome, and because leaving all three at home alone often resulted in consequences I preferred not to repeat. The community center looked entirely different in morning light — less formal, more worn around the edges, the folding chairs stacked against the wall, and the floor showing the scuff marks of decades of events that had nothing to do with murder.

Three days had passed since Vivian. The police tape had been removed from the restroom. Someone had propped a handwritten *Out of Order* sign on the door anyway, as if the room itself needed a moment.

Gerry was already there when I arrived, rearranging a table near the window. Trish had brought a tin of something that smelled like brown butter and vanilla and set it open on the refreshment table. Two women I recognized from the meeting but hadn't been introduced to were setting up chairs in a loose circle near the center of the room.

Linda appeared from the back hallway, pushing a push broom and looking genuinely pleased to see me. "You came."

"You put it in my calendar."

"I put it in your calendar because I knew you'd talk yourself out of it otherwise." She leaned the broom against the wall and crouched to greet the dogs with both hands. "How are you doing?"

"I'm fine." I handed her Minnie's leash, which she took without being asked. "Where do you need me?"

She pointed me toward the refreshment table, which suited everyone. I poured coffee, accepted a square of whatever Trish had made — shortbread, brown butter, some kind of salt on top that had no right to work as well as it did — and settled into the gradual, overlapping rhythm of a group of people who had known each other long enough to talk in half-finished sentences.

The gossip started before the chairs were fully arranged.

It always does, in rooms like this. You don't need a signal or a prompt. Someone says a name, or doesn't say it, and the conversation finds its own current.

"She'd been planning it for weeks." This came from one of the women by the chairs, Carol, I thought, or Karen. She had a Cavalier King Charles on a long lead. "The announcement. Whatever it was. She told me at the September meeting that the banquet was going to be very different this year. Her words."

"Did she say what kind of announcement?" I asked, keeping my voice neutral and my attention on my coffee.

Carol-or-Karen shook her head. "She was being mysterious about it. You know how Vivian was. She liked knowing something other people didn't. Held onto it until it would make the biggest impression."

"She told me the same thing." The second woman, older, with a Bichon and reading glasses pushed up on her head, nodded. "Said the banquet would be something no one would forget. I assumed she meant the centerpieces. She'd been arguing with the venue about the centerpieces since July."

"It wasn't centerpieces." Carol-or-Karen's voice dropped slightly in the tone of someone sharing something they'd been waiting to share. "She was unhappy about something. Something to do with the club. She'd been unhappy about it for months."

Gerry, who had finished with the table and was now pouring her own coffee, didn't turn around. But her shoulders did something. Not quite a flinch, not quite a straightening. Something in between, quickly resolved.

I watched that and said nothing.

Linda, crouched on the floor with three dachshunds orbiting her, watched Gerry too.

"The board has had a difficult year." Gerry finally turned with her coffee in both hands. "Every organization has tensions. Ours are no different."

"What kind of tensions?" I asked.

She looked at me for a moment. Not unfriendly, but more like identifying what was useful and what wasn't. "Philosophical disagreements, mostly. About the direction of the club. Membership criteria." A small pause. "Financial priorities."

"Financial," I said.

"Every club has budget discussions." She gave a warm smile, genuine in the way Gerry's smiles seemed to be, but it arrived slightly too quickly after the word 'financial' for my comfort. "We're a volunteer organization. Money is always a conversation."

Trish, who had been quietly refilling the shortbread tin, looked up. "There's an audit coming up," she said. "Routine. Completely standard. We do a financial review every two years without fail; it's in the bylaws, very straightforward. The treasurer submits everything to the outside firm, and they review it, and we get a clean report, and that's that." She placed the lid on the tin with a small, definitive click. "It's nothing."

The room had gone slightly quieter in the way rooms do when someone has used more words than the question required.

Daisy, who had been investigating the baseboard near the refreshment table, sat down and looked at Trish with her head tilted. Even my dog knew that was too much explanation for something routine.

"When is the audit?" I asked.

"End of the month." Trish smoothed the front of her apron, which didn't need smoothing. "The firm is very thorough. Very professional. We've used them for years, and they're always…it's always very clean. Very standard." She reached for the coffee carafe and refilled a cup that was already more than half full. "Vivian was on the finance committee, which is probably why people are drawing connections that aren't there. She took her committee work very seriously. Too seriously, some would say. She had opinions about how things were categorized. Accounting opinions." A small, dismissive laugh. "Not everyone agreed with her interpretations, but that's committees for you."

"What kind of interpretations?" Linda asked. She sat on the floor with Minnie in her lap now, the question delivered with the same light, conversational tone she used when she was paying the most attention.

"Accounting is very technical." Trish set the carafe down. "She thought certain expenses should be reclassified. The outside firm will review it and confirm what the rest of the committee has been saying for a year: that everything is correct, above board, and categorized appropriately. It will be fine." She picked up a dish towel. Put it down. "It's routine."

Gerry stared at Trish with an expression I couldn't fully read from across the room. Not warning exactly. Something more tired than that. The look of someone who had been watching this particular wheel turn for a while and was too worn out to stop it.

Carol-or-Karen leaned slightly toward me. "Vivian requested the audit be moved up," she said, quietly enough that it wasn't meant to carry. "It was supposed to be in the spring. She pushed for the end of the month. At the October board meeting. Apparently, it was quite the discussion."

"Quite the discussion," the woman with the Bichon repeated, with the tone of someone who knew this was an understatement on the level of calling a flood a puddle.

"She had documentation," Carol-or-Karen continued. "Nobody would say what it was, but she brought something to that meeting. Physical documents. She laid them on the table." She glanced toward Gerry, who was now discussing something with one of the volunteers near the window. "The vote to move the audit forward was three to two."

Three to two meant someone on the board had sided with Vivian. It also meant someone — two someones — had voted against her. Against moving up an audit of the club's finances. Which could mean nothing. Budget committees voted against things for procedural reasons all the time. Or it could mean something else entirely, something that had been sitting in a manila folder on a board meeting table in October and had followed Vivian into a community center restroom two days ago.

I broke off a corner of shortbread and thought about that.

I can. And I will.

She hadn't been talking about dog shows.

Linda appeared at my elbow with a coffee refill she'd gotten for me without being asked. "Vivian was on the finance committee," she said, low enough for just me. "Trish chairs the finance committee."

I looked at Trish, who was now reorganizing the refreshment table with the energy of someone who needed to be doing something with her hands. She'd straightened everything twice since we'd arrived. The shortbread tin had moved three times to different positions on the table.

"Who else is on it?" I asked.

"Colin Hart handles the show budget, so he sits in on finance meetings. Gerry as president. Vivian. And one other member who moved away in August and hasn't been replaced yet." Linda sipped her coffee. "Four people, one vacancy, and a vote that went three to two."

"Three to two with four people and one vacancy doesn't work," I said.

"No," Linda said. "It doesn't."

Which meant the vote count Carol-or-Karen had reported was either wrong or the vacancy had been filled without announcement, or there was a fifth member of the finance committee nobody had mentioned yet. Three possibilities, none of them settling.

Gerry drifted back toward the refreshment table and topped off her coffee with the ease of someone rejoining a conversation rather than entering one. "I hope you're settling in all right, Crystal. I know your introduction to the club wasn't what any of us would have wished."

"It's been memorable," I said.

She smiled, and this time it reached her eyes properly. "Vivian was difficult. I don't think anyone would argue otherwise, and I won't pretend she made my job easy. But she cared about this club. Whatever her methods, she cared." She looked at her coffee. "The announcement she'd been planning…I knew she had something in mind for the banquet. She didn't tell me the specifics. She said she wanted to handle it her way." A pause. "I should have pushed harder to know what it was."

The *should have* carried weight. "Do you have any idea what it was about?" I asked.

"I have suspicions." Gerry set down her cup. "And I intend to share them with the police at the appropriate time." She met my eyes directly, and there was something in the look that was both an answer and a boundary. *I know more than I'm saying, and I'm telling you that I know it.* "In the meantime, I'd encourage you to enjoy Trish's shortbread. She really is extraordinarily talented." She moved away with the unhurried confidence of a woman who had just said exactly as much as she intended to.

Minnie had fallen asleep in Linda's lap. Bella watched Trish with the unblinking focus she usually reserved for squirrels. Daisy had located something under the refreshment table that she found interesting and was devoting herself to it with characteristic commitment.

Trish straightened the shortbread tin one more time and didn't look up.

Chapter Seven

Saturday morning arrived with the quality of late autumn light that makes everything look slightly more significant than it is, with long shadows, gold edges, the kind of morning that encourages decisions you'd talk yourself out of by afternoon. I clipped three leashes to three collars, pocketed a bag of treats I was not supposed to have at a kennel club event, and walked my girls to Riverside Park.

Colin Hart was already there when we arrived.

He stood near the far end of the off-leash area with his hands in his jacket pockets, watching a pair of Weimaraners work the open grass. He had a travel mug and the stillness of someone who'd been there long enough to be comfortable but hadn't come for the company.

I almost turned around. Not because of him specifically, but because I'd told myself this was a walk, just a walk, and the leash untangling situation that immediately developed as Bella spotted a pigeon and

Daisy spotted Bella spotting the pigeon suggested that even a walk was going to require full managerial attention. Before I could stop them, I found myself twirling like a spinning top as I tried to get free of the leashes.

"Miss Waters." Colin had seen me. He lifted his travel mug in a minimal acknowledgment — not unfriendly, just economical, the greeting of a man who didn't waste gestures any more than he wasted words.

"Crystal." I got the dogs redirected and crossed the grass toward him. "Colin."

He looked down at the three of them with the assessing eye he'd had on the Weimaraners. "Bella's gait is good," he said. "She favors her left slightly on uneven ground. You'd want to watch that in a ring."

"She favors her left when she's thinking about something else entirely," I said. "Which in a ring would be everything."

The corner of his mouth moved. Not quite a smile, but the infrastructure of one. "They're all like that the first few times. Some of them settle. Some of them decide the audience is more interesting than the task." He glanced at Daisy, who had sat down on my foot. "She'd be a natural. She likes being looked at." He frowned. "If you could control her fuzzy hair."

This was accurate. Daisy had the specific self-possession of a dog who had never once questioned whether she was the most interesting thing in any given room.

I unclipped all three leads and let them scatter, keeping half my attention on the tree line where squirrels occasionally made poor decisions, and turned to stand beside Colin in the comfortable sideways configuration of two people who don't know each other well enough for face-to-face conversation but have found a shared direction to look.

"How long have you been a handler?" I asked.

"Fifteen years. Started with my own dogs, moved into handling for other people when word got around." He watched Minnie investigate a patch of compelling grass with the thoroughness of a forensic specialist. "I handle eight dogs currently. Sweetie Pie is the most decorated."

"Angela's Doberman."

"She's an exceptional animal." He said it with the clean, professional appreciation of someone who could separate the dog from the complicated human attached to the other end of the lead. "Angela knows what she has. She's not always easy to work with, but she takes the dog seriously, and that matters more than easy."

"Were you close to Vivian?"

The question came out more directly than I'd intended. I'd meant to approach it sideways, the way you approach a dog you don't know, letting them come to you. Instead, I'd just asked it, standing in a park on a Saturday morning with treats in my pocket and my smallest dog eating something she'd found in the grass that I was choosing not to examine.

Colin remained quiet long enough that I thought I'd miscalculated.

"We worked together," he said finally. "The show is my event. Budget, logistics, scheduling, and judging panels. That runs through the finance committee, which meant it ran through Vivian." He took a sip from his travel mug. "She was thorough. I'll say that. She knew where every dollar went, and she had opinions about where it should go instead. Working with her required patience."

"Did you have patience with her?"

Another pause. Longer this time. "Some days more than others."

I waited. Bella had abandoned the pigeon pursuit and now trotted back toward me. I scooped her up briefly, checked her paws for anything problematic, and set her back down.

"She said something to me," Colin said. "A few weeks ago, after a board meeting. I've been thinking about it since Thursday."

I kept my eyes on the dogs and said nothing, which is the correct response when someone is deciding how much to say.

"She said she expected more from me than loyalty." He turned the travel mug in his hands. "Her exact words were that I owed her more than loyalty, and that she hoped I'd remember that before the banquet." He stopped. "I've been trying to work out what she meant."

"Did you ask her?"

"I did. She smiled and changed the subject." He made a flat, humorless sound that wasn't quite a laugh. "That was Vivian's way when she had something she wanted you to think about. She'd hand you one end of the string and walk away."

More than loyalty. I turned that over. It could mean any number of things in any number of directions. Gratitude for something she'd done for him. Silence about something she knew. Cooperation with whatever announcement she'd been building toward the banquet like a slow, deliberate fire.

"Colin." I kept my voice even. "Is there anything between you and Vivian that the police should probably know about?"

He looked at me then, directly, and I met it without flinching. His expression was not the expression of a man caught at something. It was the expression of a man who had been waiting for the question and had already decided how to answer it.

"People have been saying things," he said. "I'm aware of that. In a club this size, with people who have known each other for years and not always liked what they've known, well, things get said." He looked back at the field. "There was nothing between Vivian and me. Not in the way people are implying."

"But there's a reason people are implying it."

A long moment. Daisy had found a stick three times her size and carried it with the pride of someone who'd acquired property.

"Two years ago, Vivian intervened in a situation involving the show accounts," he said. "There was a discrepancy. Not large, and not…it wasn't what it looked like, but it looked bad enough that if it had gone to the full board, my contract would have been reviewed." His jaw tightened slightly. "Vivian handled it internally. Within the finance committee. The matter was resolved without it going further."

"She protected you."

"She resolved a misunderstanding," he said carefully. "And then she held it. Not loudly. She never brought it up directly after that. But it was always there. In the way she'd look at me sometimes during meetings. In comments like the one she made after the board meeting." He exhaled. "She collected things, Vivian. People's vulnerabilities. She held them the way some people hold insurance policies. Quietly, just in case."

I thought about the manila folder on the board meeting table. The documents she'd laid out in October. A woman who collected things didn't just collect one thing.

"The night of the meeting," I said. "Before everything happened. You were near the back hallway when I went to the restroom. I noticed you coming out of the door near the office."

He looked at me with an expression that recalibrated my understanding of how carefully he'd been listening to everything I'd said since we'd arrived at this park.

"The club office," he confirmed. "Yes."

"What were you doing in there?"

"Retrieving something." He said it without evasion, which was itself a kind of evasion — answering the what without touching the why. "Private correspondence. Letters that had been filed in the club records that I had reason to believe Vivian had put there. Things between the two of us related to the account situation. I didn't want them sitting in a filing cabinet." He paused. "I went to get them back."

"Before or after you knew she was dead?"

"Before." His voice was flat and certain. "I had no idea what had happened in that restroom. I went to the office during the meeting when I thought I had a window, and I came back out, and twenty minutes later, your boyfriend arrived with half the Riverside PD." He looked at me with the level, slightly tired expression of a man who understood exactly how this sounded. "I've been deciding whether to tell the police about the letters."

"You should tell them," I said. "Whatever they say."

"I know." He didn't sound like a man who was going to do something he knew he should do. He sounded like a man still measuring the distance between should and will. "The letters don't make me look innocent, Crystal. They make me look like someone with a reason."

"You had a reason before you retrieved them," I said. "The account situation gave you that regardless. Taking the letters just adds a layer."

He was quiet for a moment, turning the travel mug again. "You're direct."

"I'm a property manager. If I weren't direct, I'd spend my entire life dancing around broken washing machines."

Something shifted in his expression, not quite relaxing, but loosening slightly at the edges. He looked out at the field, where Minnie had given up on the grass investigation and now sat in a patch of sunlight with her eyes half-closed. Bella leaped around like a ballerina as she tried to catch a butterfly. Daisy still carried her stick, hoping someone would toss it for her to fetch.

"The affair rumor," he said. "For what it's worth. It started because someone saw Vivian coming out of my car in the club parking lot after an evening meeting eight months ago. We'd had a conversation she didn't want overheard inside. That's the entirety of it." His voice was even and undefended. "She was not a woman I had feelings for. She was a woman who made my professional life complicated and then made it more complicated by resolving the thing that complicated it."

"A favor that came with a string," I said.

"A very long string." He capped his travel mug. "That she'd been winding tighter for two years."

Daisy dropped her stick at Colin's feet. He looked down at it, then crouched and threw it. She bolted after it with the full commitment of a dog who had never once doubted a stick was worth running for.

"One more question," I said. "The letters you retrieved. Were they yours, or hers?"

He straightened. Met my eyes one more time with that same measured, assessing look. "Both," he said. "That's rather the problem."

He picked up his travel mug, called a brief goodbye to Minnie, who ignored him, and crossed the grass toward the park exit with the unhurried gait of a man who had said more than he'd planned to and had made his peace with it somewhere between the stick and the question.

I stood in the autumn light with three dachshunds and a pocket full of contraband treats and thought about a filing cabinet, a pair of letters, and a woman who had spent two years collecting string.

Bella pressed against my ankle.

"I know," I said. "Here we go again."

Chapter Eight

"I really don't know how you got yourself into another murder mystery so soon." Linda shook her head as she turned into the parking lot of Carmine's Italian Eatery, which was the kind of Italian restaurant that had been in the same family for thirty years and smelled like garlic bread from the parking lot.

I wasn't part of the board. I had been a member of the Riverside Kennel Club for exactly one week and had so far attended one meeting and discovered one body, which by any reasonable metric was a full enough start. But Linda was on the volunteer committee, and the monthly board lunch apparently required her presence, and Linda without company was Linda with leverage, so here I was.

There were a million other things I'd rather be doing. The laundromat light still needed a second look, I had two tenant emails sitting unanswered in my inbox, and having lunch with a table full of murder suspects was enough to put anyone off pasta. "I didn't plan on someone being killed while I was using the restroom." I shot her a sideways glare. "Why not just be happy you aren't a suspect this time?"

"I have range," she said pleasantly. "Why did you wear a white blouse to an Italian restaurant?"

I looked down at it. "Living on the wild side." I shoved my car door open before she could say anything else, mostly because I couldn't admit that I'd been half-asleep when she called that morning and had retained approximately none of the details about where we were going. I'd heard *lunch* and had filled in the rest.

Carmine's was busy for a weekday. The lunch crowd had taken most of the front tables, and the hostess led us through to a private room in the back that the club apparently used regularly. A long table was already set, a breadbasket in the center, a carafe of water, and one of red wine that nobody had waited for permission to open

Gerry sat at the head of the table. Trish was beside her, already buttering bread with the focused pleasure of a woman who baked professionally and ate without apology. Colin was there, in the same composed stillness he'd had at the park, his jacket on the back of his chair, a glass of water in front of him untouched. Angela sat at the far end with the deliberate body language of someone who had chosen her seat to maximize distance from the rest of the table and didn't care who noticed.

Two other members I recognized from the

Thursday volunteer morning filled the middle seats. Carol, whose last name I'd since learned was Fenton, and the woman with the Bichon, whose name was Rosemary Dodd and who wore the expression of someone who came to these lunches primarily for the bread and the information, in that order.

Linda and I took the two remaining seats, which placed me directly across from Trish and one seat down from Gerry, which was either good or bad depending on how the next hour went.

The menus went around. The wine went around. Gerry asked about my dogs with the genuine warmth she seemed to extend to everyone, and Trish offered a detailed opinion on which pasta shape held cream sauce best, which was more useful information than anything else I'd gathered all week.

The murder didn't come up for the first twenty minutes, which was a record.

It was Carol who broke it, in the way Carol seemed to break most things — with the air of someone raising a topic that had been on the table the whole time, just waiting for someone brave enough to name it. "Has anyone spoken to the police again since Thursday?"

"They spoke to all of us Thursday night," Colin said, without locking up from his menu.

"I meant since then." Carol glanced around the table. "They came back to speak with me yesterday. Asked about the finance committee. About the audit."

She glanced at Trish. "I assume they came to you as well."

Trish's butter knife made a small sound against her bread plate. "Yes. It was very straightforward. I told them exactly what I told them on Thursday. The audit is routine, the committee's records are in order, and Vivian's concerns were her own interpretations, which the outside firm will address when they complete their review." She set the knife down. "I said the same thing four times in four different ways because they kept asking it in four different ways, but the answer didn't change."

"What were Vivian's concerns, exactly?" I asked.

The table went quiet in a way that told me this was not a new question but was one that nobody had yet answered in a room with multiple people present.

Gerry set her wine glass down with the deliberate care of someone making a decision. "Vivian believed that certain show expenses had been misclassified over the past two seasons. She felt they had been recorded in a way that obscured where the money was actually going. She brought documentation to the October board meeting and requested that the audit be moved forward."

"Documentation," I said.

"Spreadsheets. Receipts she'd tracked down herself. Correspondence." Gerry's voice was measured. "Vivian was meticulous when she committed to something. Whatever else she was, she was thorough."

Angela made a sound at the far end of the table that wasn't quite a word. Everyone looked at her. She picked up her wine and looked back with the flat, direct expression of a woman who had decided to be in this room but reserved the right to have feelings about it.

"She wasn't only questioning the finances," Angela said. "Let's not be selective about what we're discussing."

Gerry's expression shifted slightly. Not surprise, more the look of someone who'd known this was coming and had hoped it wouldn't arrive until after the bread course.

"She was questioning bloodlines," Angela said. "Specifically, mine. And I'm not going to sit at this table and let the finances be the headline while that gets quietly buried along with her."

The room was very still. Rosemary Dodd reached for the breadbasket.

"Sweetie Pie's bloodline is registered, documented, and verified," Angela continued. "Her sire and dam are both champion-line animals. Her papers are legitimate and have been examined by three separate registrars. What Vivian was suggesting was not only wrong, it was deliberately malicious, and she knew it."

"What was she suggesting?" I asked over the rim of my water glass.

Angela looked at me directly. "That I had falsified her registration. That her papers were altered.

That Sweetie Pie's actual parentage didn't match what was registered with the breed association." She set her glass down. "She was suggesting that every award Sweetie Pie has won was won under false pretenses. Which would mean I'm a fraud and my dog is a fraud and two years of wins should be vacated."

"Angela —" Gerry began.

"I'm not finished." Angela wasn't loud. She didn't need to be. "She made the same accusation about at least two other members of this club. I know because they called me when they found out what she was saying. She wasn't going to the banquet to make an announcement, Gerry. She was going to the banquet to make an execution. In public, in front of everyone, with whatever documents she'd collected."

The table absorbed this in silence.

I glanced at Colin, who stared at his water glass with the expression of a man keeping very careful track of something internal and not wanting to get involved in a squabble.

"Who else?" Linda asked quietly.

Angela's gaze moved briefly to Carol Fenton, who had gone slightly pink and was finding the breadbasket very interesting. Then to Rosemary Dodd, whose Bichon I was now thinking about in a new context entirely. Then, for just a fraction of a second, to Colin, before moving on.

It was a short look. The kind designed not to be noticed, but I noticed it.

"She came to me in September," Carol said finally, to the breadbasket. "She said she had reason to believe that Biscuit's registration didn't reflect his actual lineage. She said his confirmation scores were inconsistent with his registered parentage, and she'd had a specialist look at his build." She shook her head. "Biscuit is my dog. I've had him since he was eight weeks old. I was at the breeding facility. I have photographs." She looked up. "I don't know what she thought she had, but she was wrong."

"She may have been wrong," Gerry said carefully. "Or she may have been working from incomplete information. Or —" She stopped.

"Or she was right about some of it," Angela finished. "Which is what you're not saying."

Gerry looked at her wine for a moment. Then at me, with the expression she'd had at the volunteer morning. That deliberate, boundaried look that communicated *I know more than I'm saying, and I'm telling you that I know it.*

"Vivian came to me privately three weeks ago," Gerry said. "Not about bloodlines. About the finances. She said she had found irregularities she couldn't explain through any legitimate accounting interpretation. She said she had taken her concerns as far as she could within the committee and had been told they were explained. She didn't believe the explanation." A pause. "She said if the audit didn't surface what she'd found, she would take her documentation directly to the breed association and the regional show committee."

The breadbasket had stopped moving.

"Both," I said. "She was going to do both at the banquet. The bloodlines and the finances."

"That's what I believe, yes." Gerry folded her hands on the table. "Which means she had potentially given multiple people a reason to want that banquet to never arrive."

I looked around the table. Trish, who was very still in a way that was different from her Thursday stillness — less the overexplaining energy of someone managing anxiety and more the careful quiet of someone doing arithmetic. Colin, who had still not touched his water. Angela, who had said everything she'd come to say and now watched the rest of us with the attentive calm of a person who had placed a stone on a table and was waiting to see which direction it rolled. Carol, pink and unhappy. Rosemary, whose expression had the quality of someone sitting on something heavy.

The waiter appeared. Everyone ordered with the slightly automatic politeness of people performing normalcy.

When he left, Linda leaned close enough to speak under the table noise. "White blouse," she murmured. "Italian restaurant. Murder suspects. How's the wild side treating you?"

"Ask me after the pasta," I said.

Gerry caught my eye from her end of the table, and for a moment, it was just the two of us in the room, or I felt that way. "Crystal," she said, with the tone of someone choosing words the way you choose footing on uncertain ground. "I want you to know that I intend to share everything I've told you today with the police. I should have done it sooner."

"Why didn't you?" I placed my napkin in my lap, strongly suspecting I should have worn it like a bib.

She considered this with more honesty than I expected. "Because I hoped it would be simpler than it is. A crime of passion, perhaps. An argument that escalated. Something that didn't require pulling the whole fabric of this club apart to find the thread." She picked up her wine. "I don't think it's going to be that simple."

"No," I said. "I don't think so either."

Across the table, Trish reached for the breadbasket and knocked her water glass. She caught it before it spilled, righted it with both hands, and laughed a small, relieved laugh that nobody joined. Her hands were shaking.

I picked up my menu, looked at it without reading it, and thought about a woman with spreadsheets, receipts, and registered correspondence, building a case against people who had every reason to stop her, in a club where everyone kept secrets the way Vivian kept insurance — quietly, just in case.

The pasta arrived. I forked some noodles and

brought them to my mouth. They fell off the fork and onto my white blouse almost immediately.

Linda didn't say a word; instead, she ducked her head to hide a smirk. Which, from Linda, was its own kind of commentary.

Chapter Nine

The fundraiser had been Gerry's idea, or at least Gerry's solution. A bake sale and silent auction to offset the cost of the upcoming regional show, which apparently ran a larger deficit than the membership understood and a smaller one than Vivian had been claiming, depending on who you asked. The planning had stalled in the week since the murder, which was understandable, and Gerry had decided that momentum was the best available remedy for a club that was running on gossip and unease.

She'd sent an email to the full membership on Monday morning. Cheerful, purposeful, the tone of a woman steering something back toward shore. Volunteers were needed to help organize donation receipts and cross-reference them against the existing ledger before the audit. No accounting experience necessary. Just a few hours on Wednesday afternoon.

I had read the email three times. Then I'd replied before I talked myself out of it.

I left the dogs with Linda, who had offered without being asked in the way she did when she understood why I needed to go somewhere without three dachshunds pulling me toward every distraction in the room. All three dogs stared at me as if I'd betrayed them and was never coming back home.

The community center smelled like fresh coffee and cleaning product, the latter a little stronger than necessary near the hallway that still had an *Out of Order* sign on the restroom door despite the police tape being long gone. Someone kept replacing the sign. I suspected it would stay up through the new year.

Gerry had set up in the main meeting room rather than in the small office, which I noted without comment. A folding table held two cardboard boxes of receipts, a binder, a laptop, and a coffee station that had clearly been organized by someone who took coffee seriously. Three other volunteers were already seated when I arrived — Rosemary Dodd, who nodded at me; a younger woman named Patrice who handled the club's social media and had the energy of someone who processed tasks the way other people processed conversation; and an older gentleman named Howard who bred Basset Hounds and had apparently been doing the club's administrative filing since before Gerry's presidency.

Trish arrived seven minutes after I did, slightly breathless, with a second box under one arm and her oversized tote bag on the other shoulder. She set both down, shrugged off her coat, and smiled at the room with the warm, inclusive smile that I'd come to understand was her default setting. Genuine in origin but deployed so consistently that it had become a kind of armor.

"Sorry, sorry. The second batch of silent auction forms were still at the bakery. I brought everything I had." She began unloading the box. "Gerry, I have the October donor forms and the September auction receipts. I think once we cross-reference those against the ledger, we'll have everything the auditors need for that portion."

Gerry looked up from the laptop. "Wonderful. Howard, would you pull the ledger from the binder? We'll start with July and work forward."

Howard opened the binder and flipped through the tabbed sections, then stopped. He flipped back. Forward again. Then he looked up with the mild, unconcerned expression of someone who hadn't yet decided whether what he was seeing was a problem.

"July, August, October, November." He looked at Gerry. "September isn't here."

The room didn't react dramatically. Nobody gasped. It was more a stillness that descends when something small turns out to matter.

Gerry frowned and leaned over to look for herself. "That can't be right. The ledger sections are filed monthly without exception. It's been the same system for six years." She checked the tabs herself. Howard was correct. September was simply absent — the binder moved from August to October as if the intervening month had decided not to happen.

"I have it," Trish said quickly. She was still organizing the forms from her box and didn't look up immediately. "I took it home. Last month. I was reconciling the summer show expenses, and it was easier to work from home, so I brought it with me. I must have forgotten to return it." She looked up then and smiled. "I'll bring it on Thursday. It's not a problem."

It was a perfectly reasonable explanation. Volunteer treasurers worked from home all the time. Taking a ledger to reconcile accounts outside of office hours was standard practice for any committee operating on donated time. There was nothing about what she'd said that was factually implausible.

Except that her smile was a fraction too tight. Not by much. Someone who didn't know her well might not have caught it. Might have seen Trish's usual warmth, accepted the explanation, and moved on to the October receipts. But I'd watched her at the volunteer morning, and at the Italian restaurant, and I'd catalogued the specific register of her smiles the way you catalogue things that turn out to matter later. The smile she gave the shortbread tin and the smile she gave a question she wasn't comfortable with were different animals, and this was the second one.

"Of course," Gerry said. "We can work around

September for now. Patrice, can you start entering the October donor information while we sort the auction receipts by date?"

Work redistributed. Conversation resumed at the low, productive murmur of people doing tasks. Howard filed. Rosemary sorted. Patrice typed.

I took a seat near the receipt boxes and began working through the silent auction forms, which were straightforward. Donor name, item description, estimated value, and final bid amount. Someone had organized them loosely by category and then abandoned the system halfway through, which meant they needed to be resorted before entry. I didn't mind. Sorting gave me something to do with my hands and an excuse to move through the documents slowly.

Trish settled across from me with the October donor forms and her own pile to work through. For a while, neither of us said anything, and the room was comfortable enough that silence didn't require explanation.

"These are lovely donations," Trish offered, after ten minutes or so. "The Hendersons gave a weekend at their lake house again. That always does well at auction."

"It sounds like it would." I held up a form. "What does this notation mean? There's an asterisk next to this donation and a handwritten note I can't quite read."

She leaned across to look. "In-kind donation. It means the item was donated rather than purchased by the club. The asterisk flags it for the auditors so they can classify it correctly." She sat back. "Vivian came up with that system. She was very particular about in-kind versus cash value classifications."

"She seems to have been particular about a lot of things."

"She was." Trish's voice was neutral and careful, the tone of someone paying a compliment they didn't feel while avoiding a criticism they did. "She had strong opinions about how the books should reflect the club's activity. Not everyone agreed with her methodology."

"Did you?"

A brief pause. Trish smoothed a form that didn't need smoothing. "We had different approaches. I've been managing volunteer accounts for fifteen years across three different organizations, and there are established ways of doing things that work and that auditors understand. Vivian wanted everything reclassified according to her own system, which would have required us to restate two years of accounts." She looked up. "That's not a minor undertaking. It creates confusion, it raises flags, and it doesn't change the underlying numbers. It just changes how they're labeled."

"Unless the relabeling changes what the numbers appear to show," I said.

It came out more directly than I'd planned. I'd been aiming for neutral and landed somewhere slightly past it. Trish looked at me with an expression that moved through several things quickly — recognition, assessment, something careful — before settling back into the warmth she wore as standard.

"Accounting isn't as dramatic as people make it sound," she said. "Classifications exist on a spectrum. Reasonable people disagree about where things belong. That's why audits exist. To have an independent professional confirm that the approach is sound."

"And if the independent professional agrees with Vivian's interpretation instead of yours?"

Silence. Howard had asked Rosemary something at the other end of the table, and they were engaged in their own quiet exchange. Gerry was on the phone near the door. Nobody was paying attention to the two of us.

Trish set the form she was holding down. She looked at her hands for a moment, then at me, with an expression that had dropped the extra layer. Not unfriendly, but unguarded in a way I hadn't seen from her before, as if she'd decided something.

"The auditors will look at the accounts, and they'll find what's there to find," she said quietly. "Whatever Vivian thought she had, whatever interpretation she preferred, the firm will make their own determination. That's how it works."

"What happens if they find something that supports her position?" I tilted my head.

"Then the board will address it." She picked up the form again. "That's also how it works."

It was a composed, rational answer. It was also an answer that hadn't addressed what I'd actually asked: what would happen to Trish specifically if the audit confirmed that Vivian had been right. That was the question she'd moved around.

I went back to the auction forms. Three more with asterisks, all correctly notated, all from September. Which meant that whoever had handled the September receipt documentation had also handled the September ledger, and the September ledger was currently sitting in Trish's house, and the audit was at the end of the month.

Gerry returned from her phone call, refilled her coffee, and asked whether anyone needed anything, and the room resumed its productive murmur. Trish smiled at something Rosemary said. Howard found an inconsistency in the November filing and flagged it with a sticky note. Patrice typed.

I sorted receipts and watched Trish the way Bella watched things she hadn't categorized yet. Quietly, from a slight distance, waiting to see what they did when they thought nobody was paying attention.

At half past three, when the afternoon's work was winding down and people were gathering their things, I helped Gerry stack the finished binders at the end of the table.

"Thank you for coming," she said, quietly enough not to carry. "I mean that."

"Of course." I straightened the binder stack and

kept my voice equally low. "Gerry. The September ledger. When did Trish say she took it home?"

Gerry looked at me steadily. "She said last month. During the summer show reconciliation."

"The summer show reconciliation would have been August at the latest," I said. "September's receipts wouldn't have been in a September ledger until September was over. Which means she couldn't have taken it home during the summer reconciliation. She'd have taken it in October at the earliest."

Gerry held my gaze for a moment. The afternoon light through the community center windows had gone low and flat, the way late autumn light does when the day is finishing without ceremony.

"Yes," she said. "I noticed that too."

She picked up her coat and her bag and went to thank the volunteers, and I stood at the end of the table with a binder in my hands, feeling like a piece that fit somewhere important, but I hadn't yet found the edge it belonged to.

Outside, a car started in the parking lot. Inside, Trish laughed at something Howard said, warm, easy, and completely natural.

I put the binder down and went to get my coat. What was really going on at the kennel club?

Chapter Ten

"Crystal."

The voice came from somewhere below and behind me, and my arms windmilled from the top of the ladder before I'd fully processed whose voice it was or what it had said. The light bulb — the whole reason I was eight feet off the ground on a Tuesday afternoon — left my hand in the same moment my balance left me, and I had a brief, weightless second of clarity in which I understood exactly what was about to happen before I bounced down the rungs and landed at Lance's feet with an impact that I would be feeling in just about every inch of my body.

The bulb, miraculously, did not shatter. It rolled under the nearest washing machine and disappeared.

"I didn't mean to startle you." Lance crouched and held out a hand. "Are you hurt?"

"Just some bruises." I took his hand and let him pull me upright, doing my best to inventory the damage without making it obvious. Both knees. Left hip. Some portion of my dignity. "You shouldn't sneak up on people."

"I didn't." He pointed at my ears. "You couldn't hear me."

I removed the earbuds. The sounds of the laundromat filled in around me. The mechanical hum of the working machines, the distant clank of the faulty dryer I had on my list for Thursday, the faint smell of detergent that lived permanently in the walls. "How long were you standing there?"

"Long enough to say your name three times."

I straightened my tool belt and decided not to pursue that line. The ladder was still upright against the wall, which was better than it could have been. The bulb was gone. I'd need to move the washing machine to get it back, which meant that the problem had officially grown in the time it took me to fall off a ladder.

"Can we talk?" He gestured toward the bench along the far wall, where people sat and waited for their laundry.

"Sure." I followed him without moving as fast as I normally would, because my left hip had now registered its full opinion of the last sixty seconds. "Must be serious if you're stopping by during a shift."

He sat. I sat beside him, and the bench was more welcome than I would have admitted. He had his jacket on, which meant he'd come from somewhere official or was going somewhere official. "We've spoken to all of the kennel club members. Some more than once."

"I assumed you had."

"They've mentioned that you're volunteering. Going over receipts with the fundraiser committee." He didn't phrase it as a question, which meant he already knew the answer and had come to say something about it rather than confirm the fact.

"I'm a member. Members volunteer." I kept my voice reasonable. "There's no crime in helping sort donation forms."

"There is when one of the people at the table is a killer." His voice rose slightly, and he took a breath and brought it back down with visible effort. "Crystal. We talked about this."

"We talked about me being careful. I'm being careful."

He sighed. "The autopsy report came back."

I turned to face him more fully. The laundromat machine nearest us moved into its spin cycle, and the bench vibrated faintly with it.

"She was struck from behind," he said. "Single blow, significant force, the dispenser you identified. She likely went down immediately. The knife was postmortem." He paused. "Based on lividity and the medical examiner's assessment of the blood pooling, the blow occurred approximately four to five minutes after the first set of footsteps we can account for leaving the restroom."

Four to five minutes. I'd told him in the restroom

that night — four or five minutes after Angela left and before the second person entered. I'd been sitting in a locked stall counting time by sound with nothing else to do, so the estimate was as reliable as anything I had.

"So, Angela left," I said slowly. "And whoever came in second waited. Or was already in the building and timed it."

"That's one interpretation."

"What's another?"

"That the timing is coincidental and Angela came back." He said it in the careful, neutral tone of a detective presenting possibilities rather than conclusions. "We haven't ruled her out."

"She was sick," I said. "When the room filled up, she went straight into a stall. You don't fake that."

"No," he said. "You don't, but she could have felt remorse."

The spin cycle finished. The machine clicked into silence and the laundromat settled back into its baseline hum. Through the window, I could see the common area of Riverside Towers going about its afternoon: Mrs. Henderson on her bench with a paperback, a maintenance van from the crew I'd hired parked near the east entrance, a pair of pigeons conducting their own investigation near the mailboxes.

Ordinary Tuesday. Ordinary world, existing alongside the considerably less ordinary thing that had taken up residence in the back of my mind for the better part of two weeks.

"Are you sure you didn't recognize the second voice?" Lance asked. "Anything at all. A tone, an accent, a speech pattern."

I thought about it — not trying to force it, just opening the door and seeing what was there. The sound had been soft. Deliberate. "It wasn't distinctive. If anything, that was the thing. It was too controlled. Too quiet for a normal conversation. You don't whisper to someone you're not afraid of being overheard with."

"Which suggests they knew someone might be listening," Lance said.

"Or they didn't want Vivian to hear them coming." I let that sit for a moment. "From behind, you said. Vivian was struck from behind. So, she wasn't facing whoever it was. Maybe she didn't know who came in."

Lance wrote something in his notebook, which he'd produced at some point without my noticing. "You stayed in the stall the whole time. Even after the thud."

"I didn't come out until things had been quiet long enough that I thought it was safe." I looked at my hands. There was a grease smear on my left palm from the ladder rung, and I rubbed at it absently. "I know it sounds cowardly."

"It sounds sensible." His voice had shifted — less detective, more Lance. "If you'd come out, there's a reasonable chance we wouldn't be having this conversation." He said it the way people say true things they'd rather not say, flat and careful and meaning every word.

I knew he was right. I also knew that knowing someone is right and sitting comfortably with the thing they're right about were different experiences, and I hadn't entirely managed the second one yet. "There's something I should have told you sooner."

He waited.

"Wednesday. At the volunteer session. We were cross-referencing the receipts against the club ledger. Howard went to pull it from the binder, and September was missing. The whole month."

Lance's pen stilled. "Missing how?"

"Just absent. The binder goes July, August, October. September isn't there." I watched his face. "Trish said she'd taken it home during the summer show reconciliation. That she'd forgotten to return it."

"But?"

"The summer show reconciliation would have been August at the latest. September's receipts and entries wouldn't exist until September was over, which means she couldn't have taken a September ledger home in August. The earliest she could have taken it would have been October." I kept my voice even. "Gerry noticed it too. She confirmed it to me at the end of the session."

Lance wrote more in his notebook. Faster, closer together, the shorthand of someone getting something down before the shape of it shifted. "Why didn't you tell me this immediately?"

"I was going to. Then you showed up, and I fell off a ladder, and it took me a moment to get organized." I gestured at my general situation as supporting evidence.

He looked up. The detective expression and the other one were doing complicated negotiations behind his eyes. "Trish Donnelly chairs the finance committee."

"She does."

"Vivian was on the finance committee."

"Also correct."

"Vivian was pushing for a reclassification of accounts that Trish opposed. She brought documentation to the board meeting in October. She had what Gerry described as physical documents." He said it as if he were following a thread, not asking me to confirm what he already knew. "And the month that's currently missing from the club records is the month between the summer show, which is where the expense discrepancies reportedly originate, and the October meeting where Vivian laid out her case."

"September," I said. "The bridge between what happened and when Vivian proved it."

He closed the notebook. "Crystal."

"I know."

"I'm not saying this to be difficult." He turned to face me more directly, and the official layer was entirely gone now, which was sometimes harder to deal with than the detective. "Someone in that club hit a woman in the back of the head hard enough to kill her. That person sat at your lunch table. They helped you sort receipts. They know you were in that restroom, and they know you heard something, and now you're in the middle of the documentation that may or may not tell the whole story about why Vivian died." He held my gaze. "The September ledger is missing. If someone took it, they took it for a reason. And if they find out that you've noticed it's gone —"

"Gerry noticed it first," I said. "In front of the whole room."

"Gerry isn't the one who fell into a murder investigation by accident and then started volunteering for the suspect committee."

"I prefer to think of it as the fundraiser committee."

He didn't smile. "Crystal."

"I heard you," I said. And I had. I'd heard every word. "I'll be careful."

"You said that last time."

"And I was. I'm still here." I stood, slowly, because my hip had firm opinions about the pace of things. "I'll stay out of the receipts. I'll let you handle the ledger." I looked at him. "But Lance — Gerry knows something. More than she's said to either of us. She's been deciding when and how to say it, and I think the ledger conversation may have moved the timeline." I picked up my tool belt from the bench. "She trusts me. She might tell me before she tells you."

He stood beside me and remained quiet for a moment. Around us, the laundromat hummed and clicked and smelled of detergent and the particular closeness of useful, unglamorous spaces.

"If she says anything," he said at last, with the resignation of a man making a concession he'd already known he was going to make, "you tell me immediately."

"Immediately," I agreed.

He looked at the washing machine hiding my light bulb. Then at the ladder. Then at me. "Do you want help moving that?"

"Yes," I said. "But don't say my name while I'm on it."

Chapter Eleven

Lance called at seven-fifteen on Thursday morning, which was early enough that I was still in the negotiation phase of getting out of bed. The phase where Bella is pressed against one side and Minnie against the other, and Daisy has arranged herself across my feet, and the combined weight of three dachshunds creates a compelling argument for staying exactly where you are indefinitely.

I answered on the second ring.

"I need you to come in," he said. "This morning, if you can."

"To the station?"

"Yes."

He didn't offer more than that, which, with Lance, meant either he couldn't say over the phone or he was still deciding how much to say at all. Both possibilities were enough to get me out of bed, which the dachshunds registered as a personal betrayal before relocating to the warm space I'd left.

I called Linda on the way out, and she appeared at my door eleven minutes later with the quiet promptness of someone who had been waiting to be useful. She took the leashes without being asked, told me to call her when I was done, and I left Riverside Towers with the feeling of a morning that had already decided to be significant.

Lance met me in the hallway outside the small conference room they used for non-interrogation interviews, the one with the rectangular table and the window that looked onto the parking lot. He had a coffee in each hand and the carefully neutral expression that meant he had something to show me and had already thought through how I was going to react to it.

"Sit down," he said. "Please."

I sat. He placed the coffee in front of me and opened the laptop already on the table, angling it so we could both see the screen.

"We pulled footage from the community center's security system," he said. "Interior hallway cameras. The quality is what you'd expect from a system that was installed a decade ago and hasn't been updated since."

The footage was grainy. Washed out in the over-lit sections, murky in the corners, the timestamp in the lower right corner was rendered in a pixelated font that looked like something from a gas station receipt. The angle covered the hallway that ran between the main meeting room and the corridor where the restrooms and the club office were located. It was the same hallway I'd walked down that night, past the bulletin board with its obedience class flyers and the notice about the missing Cavalier.

Lance reached over and pressed play.

The hallway was empty for a moment. Then motion. A figure moved from the meeting room end of the corridor toward the restrooms with a stride I recognized before the resolution gave me any detail to work with. The posture was unmistakable. Angular, controlled, the walk of a woman entirely comfortable with being watched. Angela Merritt, Sweetie Pie, nowhere in evidence, heading toward the restroom with the directness of someone who knew where she was going and how long she intended to be there.

The timestamp read 7:43 PM.

"That's Angela going in," Lance said. "We have her on this corridor again, four minutes and twenty seconds later, coming back out. She doesn't appear distressed. She walks at the same pace. She turns back toward the meeting room."

He let the footage run. The hallway emptied again. A minute passed on the timestamp. A minute thirty. I watched the pixelated corridor and thought about sitting in a locked stall, listening to footsteps, a faucet, and the sound of something that hadn't been right.

Then movement again.

A figure entered the corridor from the meeting room end, moving with less certainty than Angela had. Not hesitant exactly. More like the pace of whose stated purpose for being in the hallway was functional rather than directed. The build was softer, the clothing lighter in color against the grainy background, and the figure paused once, briefly, to look back the way they'd come before continuing toward the restroom corridor and passed out of the camera's frame.

I looked at Lance. He looked at the screen.

"What's the timestamp?" I asked, though I could read it myself.

"Seven forty-nine. Six minutes after Angela came back out." He paused the footage. "That's Trish Donnelly."

I sat with that for a moment. The coffee in front of me was untouched and growing cool, and I didn't reach for it. Six minutes after Angela left. The timeline the autopsy had given, plus a few seconds. Four to five minutes between Angela's departure and the blow that killed Vivian. Trish appearing on camera at seven forty-nine placed her in that corridor inside the window. Well inside it.

"Did you speak to her about it?" I asked.

"Yesterday afternoon." He leaned back in his chair. "She confirmed she was in the hallway. She said she was looking for paper towels. That the dispenser in the meeting room kitchenette had run out, and she went to check the supply closet near the restrooms."

"Was that true? Was the dispenser empty?"

"We checked. The dispenser in the kitchenette holds a reserve roll behind the primary. It wasn't empty."

"Did she know you'd checked?"

"She does now."

I looked at the paused frame. Trish, caught mid-corridor in eight-bit resolution, heading toward a woman she had documented reasons to fear and an audit she had reasons to want controlled. A missing ledger that couldn't have gone home when she said it did. A finance committee she chaired and a classification dispute that had been escalating for a year.

"Play it again," I said.

He did. I watched Trish enter the corridor, cross toward the restroom end, and disappear from frame. The pause at the turn, the glance back. I watched it twice more.

"She's not distressed," I said.

"No."

"She doesn't look like someone going to find paper towels. She looks like someone going somewhere specific without wanting to appear that way." I considered how to say the next part. "If I were going somewhere I didn't want to be seen going, I'd walk exactly like that. Not fast enough to attract attention, a reason ready in case anyone asked, one look back to confirm nobody was watching too closely."

Lance said nothing, which meant he'd arrived at the same place and was letting me find it myself.

"The timing," I said. "Angela goes in at seven

forty-three and comes out at seven forty-seven, four minutes later. Trish appears on camera at seven forty-nine." I looked at him. "Two minutes after Angela comes out. Two minutes is enough time to confirm the corridor is clear. Enough time to check that the meeting room has resettled and that nobody is tracking the exits."

"It's also enough time to go get paper towels."

"Except the paper towels weren't needed." I pulled the coffee toward me. "Did she say anything else? When you told her the kitchenette dispenser wasn't empty?"

"She said she must have been mistaken about which one she was checking. That she got confused in the moment." He paused. "She was very calm."

"She's always very calm," I said. "Except when she's not, and then she organizes things and refills cups that don't need refilling and moves the shortbread tin around." I thought about the volunteer morning, the Italian restaurant, and the fundraiser session. "She overexplains when she's managing something. But she doesn't fall apart. She's been managing this for a while."

"Managing what, specifically?"

I looked at him. "I don't know exactly. That's your job." I paused. "But the September ledger and this footage are pointing in the same direction, Lance. She was in that corridor in the window that the autopsy gave you. She has documentation missing that covers the period Vivian was building her case from. And her explanation for being in that hallway doesn't hold up."

"None of that is evidence of murder."

"No," I agreed. "But it's a lot of things that need explaining, and the explanations she's giving aren't the right shape."

He turned the laptop slightly and looked at the frozen frame again. Trish, mid-corridor, between the meeting room and wherever she was actually going. "There's no footage inside the restrooms," he said. "There wouldn't be. The corridor camera covers the approach but not the entry. We have her going toward that end of the hall. We don't have her going in."

"Do you have her coming back out?"

A pause that told me the answer before he gave it. "The footage has a gap. Seven fifty-one to seven fifty-eight. Camera malfunction. The system has a documented history of intermittent recording failures. The overnight log shows two other gaps earlier in the evening."

Seven minutes. Long enough. The specific kind of coincidence that you couldn't prove wasn't a coincidence and couldn't entirely trust wasn't something else. "Did you look at who had access to the camera system?"

"We're looking at it." His tone indicated that this line of inquiry had either just opened or was more complicated than a yes or no answer. He closed the laptop. "Crystal. I need to ask you something, and I need a straight answer."

"You usually do."

"At the fundraiser receipt session. When the September ledger came up." He watched my face. "How did Trish react when Howard said it was missing? Before she gave the explanation."

I thought back. The community center table, the binder open in Howard's hands, the mild look on his face as he went back and forth between August and October. The moment before Trish spoke. "She was already looking at Howard when he noticed," I said slowly. "She didn't look surprised. She looked —" I tried to find the precise word, the one that matched what I'd seen rather than what I was now primed to see. "Ready. Like she'd been waiting for it to come up and had the answer prepared."

"You're sure?"

"I noticed the smile before I heard the explanation," I said. "That's what made me clock it as wrong. The sequence was off. Most people look surprised first, then explain. She was already in the explanation."

Lance wrote something down. Outside the conference room window, a patrol car pulled into the lot. An ordinary Thursday at the Riverside PD, moving alongside the thing that had arrived in the back of my mind and taken up permanent residence.

"What happens now?" I asked.

"We bring her back in." He capped his pen. "With the footage and the ledger discrepancy, we have enough to push harder on the timeline."

"She'll have an explanation for the footage," I said. "She'll have thought of one already. She's been thinking about this since before the meeting."

"Probably." He stood and collected the laptop. "That's not necessarily a problem. People who have been constructing explanations for a while tend to overcommit to them. They fill in details that an innocent person wouldn't need to fill in." He glanced at me. "You've actually seen that yourself, from the other side of the table."

I had. I thought of the shortbread tin, which had been moved three times to three different positions on a table that didn't require it. The coffee carafe refilling a cup that was already full. The smile deployed a half-second too early, fitted over an answer that had been waiting since before the question was asked.

"She's going to say she panicked," I said. "About being seen on the footage. That she didn't want to look suspicious, so she gave an explanation without thinking it through."

"Yes," Lance said. "She probably will."

"And if that's all it is?"

He picked up his jacket from the back of his chair. "Then she panicked and gave a bad explanation, and the audit will tell us whatever the audit tells us, and the missing ledger will turn up in her house and confirm what she said, and we'll be looking somewhere else." He looked at me. "But the footage puts her in that corridor. And the timeline fits. And the paper towels weren't needed." He paused at the door. "That's enough to have a more serious conversation."

I stood and picked up my coffee, cold now and half-full. Through the window, the patrol car had parked and gone quiet.

"Lance." He turned. "The camera gap. Seven fifty-one to seven fifty-eight." I held his gaze. "Someone found Vivian at seven fifty-nine. That's when the room filled up. That's when everything started."

"I know," he said. "Believe me. I know."

Chapter Twelve

I was already late for my volunteer shift at the kennel club, but I needed to mentally sort through some things before entering the lion's den again. So, I sat on my sofa, coffee forgotten on the table in front of me.

Minnie stretched out alongside my left thigh with the long-suffering contentment of a dog who considered the sofa her primary residence and my presence on it a bonus. Bella had curled herself into the hollow between my knees, a warm, compact weight that shifted every few minutes as she resettled into a slightly different configuration of perfect. Daisy lay on her back in my arms with all four legs in the air, eyes half-closed, submitting to chest scratches with the boneless abandon of a dog who had fully surrendered to the morning.

I should've been content, comfortable, but something wasn't adding up.

I'd been turning the pieces over for days — the footage, the ledger, the too-tight smile, the explanation that arrived before the question — and they all pointed in the same direction, which should have felt like progress. It didn't. It felt like a puzzle that was mostly assembled but missing the center, the part that made everything else make sense. I had Trish in the corridor. I had a September ledger that couldn't have gone home when she said it did. I had a camera gap timed to the minute of discovery and an audit she'd described as routine.

What I didn't have was the thing that connected motive to moment. The specific thing Vivian had found, or planned to say, or had already set in motion that made the banquet announcement worth preventing by any means necessary.

My nerves twanged like a guitar playing a country western song.

A knock at the door made me jump hard enough to disturb all three dogs, who responded by storming the door and barking with the collective conviction of animals who had decided something monstrous was on the other side. Bella, despite having been asleep ten seconds earlier, led the charge with the territorial authority of a dog six times her size. Minnie contributed volume. Daisy barked once for form and then looked back at me to confirm she'd done her part.

I checked the peephole. Linda, in a yellow jacket, holding a travel mug and looking mildly entertained by the noise on my side of the door.

Not a monster. I opened it.

"Good morning." She smiled and stepped inside.

"Are you ready? Gerry said we're welcome to bring the dogs. It is a kennel club, after all. No one will mind and this way they're not home alone all day."

"Give me a minute." I reached for the harnesses hanging by the door, and the moment the dogs identified what I was holding, the room reorganized itself around the information. Minnie began spinning in tight circles with the ecstatic urgency of a dog who had been waiting for exactly this and could not believe it was finally happening. Daisy, who loved walks but harbored complicated feelings about the harness, immediately flopped onto her dog bed and sat in it, her expression one of passive protest. Bella turned and darted down the hall.

"Is it always this involved?" Linda picked up Daisy's harness and looked at it.

"Every single time." I got Minnie's on first because she was spinning past me at regular intervals, and it was mostly a matter of timing. Linda managed Daisy with the patient competence of a professional dog walker, who understood that the trick was to make the harness boring rather than exciting. I went in search of Bella.

She was under the blankets on my bed, a small but unmistakable lump approximately two-thirds of the way down, and remaining motionless. In her mind, if she didn't move, I couldn't find her.

I sat on the edge of the bed and reached under the blanket. What followed was less a harness fitting and more something resembling a wrestle with an alligator.

"Got her." I emerged slightly rumpled, Bella tucked under my arm.

Ten minutes after we should have left, all three were loaded into their car baskets and I was in the driver's seat, clicking my seatbelt with the mild exhaustion of someone who had already completed a significant task before nine in the morning.

"I'm always tired before we even get anywhere," I said.

"But you love it." Linda settled her travel mug in the cupholder.

"Completely."

The kennel club's volunteer space was the community center's side room, smaller than the main meeting room and better lit, with a row of windows that faced the parking lot and a long table that had become the unofficial home base for whatever the current administrative project happened to be. Today, it held a laptop, three-ring binders, a fresh coffee station that I strongly suspected Trish had organized, and a cardboard box with *ARCHIVED — DO NOT DISCARD* written on the side in red marker in handwriting I didn't recognize.

The dogs settled under the table with varying degrees of grace. Minnie went immediately to sleep. Daisy investigated the perimeter and found it acceptable. Bella positioned herself against my ankle and monitored the room.

Gerry was already there, as always. She had the laptop open and reading glasses on. She glanced up when we came in, smiled at the dogs with genuine warmth, and gestured toward the coffee.

Trish arrived eight minutes later, slightly pink-cheeked from a cool breeze that had started up, with a tin that released the smell of something warm and spiced when she set it on the table. Cardamom, maybe. Brown sugar. She opened it and offered it around without preamble, which was such a thoroughly Trish thing to do that it almost functioned as its own kind of cover. Hard to look at someone as a suspect when they're holding a tin of homemade pastries.

Almost.

We'd been working for forty minutes — Gerry sorting correspondence, Linda and I cross-referencing the October auction forms against Patrice's entry spreadsheet, Trish managing the incoming sponsorship documentation, when Gerry made a small sound. Not quite a word. The kind of sound a person makes when something on a screen confirms something they'd rather it hadn't.

Everyone looked at her.

"I've been going through Vivian's sent folder," Gerry said. She took her reading glasses off and held them loosely in one hand, a gesture I'd come to associate with her thinking rather than speaking. "The club account. The board asked me to review her correspondence after —" She stopped. Started again.

"We needed to know what she'd been communicating externally. To the audit firm, to the breed association."

"And?" I asked.

Gerry set the glasses on the table. "There's an email she sent two days before the meeting. Before she died." She cleared her throat and looked at the screen. "She contacted the audit firm directly. Not through the normal committee process — directly, herself, from the club account. She requested that the scope of the upcoming audit be expanded." She paused. "Significantly expanded. She wanted them to go back three years, not two. And she requested that the review include not just the general accounts but the show budget line items specifically. Handler fees. Vendor contracts. Equipment purchases."

The room got very quiet. Under the table, Bella shifted against my ankle.

"Who did she copy?" Trish asked.

I kept my eyes on my paperwork.

"Two people," Gerry said. "You and I, Trish."

A silence that had a specific shape to it. Not the absence of sound but the presence of something nobody was ready to name.

"I remember that email," Gerry said. "I received it two days before the meeting and I assumed it was related to the sponsorship contract review. We'd been discussing renegotiating two of the major sponsor agreements, and I thought the expanded scope was about that. I intended to discuss it with the committee at the meeting." She paused. "I didn't get the chance."

I studied Trish. She was focused on the sponsorship documents in front of her.

"Trish," Gerry said, carefully. "Did you respond to it?"

"No." She turned a page. "I saw it and assumed it was routine. An abundance of caution on Vivian's part. She was always expanding scope on things." A small, even laugh. "She once requested that we audit the coffee fund."

"This wasn't the coffee fund," Gerry said.

"No." Trish set down her page. "It wasn't." She looked up. "I didn't respond because I agreed with the expansion in principle and assumed it would be discussed at the meeting. Since it wasn't, and since Vivian —" She stopped. "Since everything happened, I assumed the audit firm would proceed with the original scope. I didn't think to follow up."

"You didn't mention it," Gerry said. "When we discussed the audit afterward. When the police were asking about Vivian's committee work. You didn't mention that she'd sent this email."

"It didn't seem relevant." Trish's voice was steady. "You didn't mention it, either. It was a scoping question. An internal communication. I didn't think —"

"She copied two people," I said. "You and Gerry. Gerry thought it was about sponsorship contracts. You thought it was routine." I kept my voice conversational, the tone of someone thinking out loud rather than pressing. "But she didn't copy the full committee. She didn't copy Colin, who manages the show budget. She sent it to the two people on the committee with the most oversight authority, two days before a meeting where she'd already announced she had something significant to say." I looked at Trish. "That's not routine. That's specific."

Trish looked at me for a long moment. The pastry tin sat between us, open, smelling of cardamom and brown sugar. Daisy had emerged from under the table and sat beside Trish's chair looking up at her with the expectant expression she reserved for people she'd identified as potential treat sources.

"I don't know what you're implying," Trish said.

"I'm not implying anything." I turned back to the auction forms. "I'm just noting that she chose carefully who she told and what she told them. And that, two days later, she was dead."

Gerry had put her reading glasses back on. She stared again at the laptop screen. "I need to forward this to the police." It wasn't a question, and it wasn't directed at anyone specifically. She stated it the way you state a decision once it's been made. "This afternoon."

"Of course," Trish said smoothly. "Whatever helps."

She picked up her page and continued reading. Her hands were perfectly steady.

Under the table, Bella's small, warm weight

pressed against my ankle, and I reached down and touched the top of her head briefly without looking away from the form in front of me, and thought about a woman who had known exactly who to tell and what to tell them, two days before someone made sure she couldn't say any of it out loud.

Linda refilled my coffee without being asked.

The morning continued around us, and nobody said anything more about the email. The cardamom aroma from the tin was warm and close, entirely at odds with everything else in the room.

I slipped the cookie tin into my bag. I had an idea.

Chapter Thirteen

I stayed up late baking cookies, which was either a productive use of insomnia or a sign that I'd lost perspective on how normal people spent their evenings. The dogs supervised from their beds in the kitchen doorway with the attentive authority of a quality-control panel, and by eleven o'clock the apartment smelled like brown butter and chocolate, and I had two dozen cookies cooling on the counter and a plan I was choosing not to examine too closely.

The next morning, I gave half of them to Lance, who opened the container at the door with the slightly bewildered expression of a man not accustomed to being handed baked goods at seven-fifteen AM. He'd been working late most of this week, and I hadn't seen enough of him.

"These are good," he said, after eating one in approximately two bites.

"Don't sound so surprised."

"I'm not surprised." He kissed my forehead. "I'm impressed. There's a difference."

He took them to work, and I packaged the rest in Trish's tin, which I had in fact slipped into my bag at the volunteer session. Not accidentally, but with the intention of using it as a reason to appear at her door. It wasn't my most sophisticated plan. It was, however, the only one I had.

I told my girls to behave and that I'd be back soon. Three pairs of eyes tracked me to the door with the mournful attention of dogs who took departures personally. Bella sat perfectly still with the expression of a small, judgmental saint. Minnie's ears drooped. Daisy's dark eyes spoke of betrayal.

"I'll take you for a long walk when I get back," I said. "All three of you. The long way around."

The looks on their faces said they found this insufficient.

I closed the door anyway.

Trish lived twelve minutes from Riverside Towers in a neighborhood of older craftsman houses with deep front porches and mature trees that had dropped most of their leaves by now, leaving the yards scattered with the remains in a way that was either charming or in need of raking, depending on your perspective. Her house was yellow — a warm, saturated yellow, with white trim and a hydrangea bed along the porch that had gone woody and grey for the season. Window boxes. A wreath on the door that hadn't been updated from fall to the approach of winter yet. The house of a woman who paid attention to things and sometimes ran slightly behind.

I rang the doorbell. Waited. Rang it again.

Nothing moved inside that I could hear, and the curtains on the front window were drawn to within an inch or two of each other, leaving a narrow gap. I leaned slightly toward it, not fully, not with intent, just the natural inclination of a person standing close to a window, wondering if anyone was home.

A pair of eyes blinked back at me from the gap.

I gasped, stumbled backward off the porch step, and landed squarely in the hydrangea bush with the tin of cookies clutched against my chest like I was protecting it from impact. The branches were dry and scratchy and not remotely forgiving, and for a moment, I just lay there in the hydrangeas looking up at the November sky and accepting the situation.

The front door opened.

"Crystal?" Trish appeared on the porch in an apron, both hands extended, her expression caught between alarm and the involuntary pull of something she was working not to find funny. "Are you all right?"

"Fine." I took her hand, and she hauled me upright. "Scratches. Nothing that matters." I extracted a hydrangea twig from my hair and held out the tin. "I accidentally slipped this into my bag yesterday. I wanted to return it and made you cookies to make up for it."

The frown that crossed her face was brief. A single second of something that might have been calculation before the warmth moved back in and replaced it so smoothly that if I hadn't been watching, I'd have missed it entirely.

"How thoughtful." She accepted the tin and held the door open. "Come in. I just made coffee. We can have a cup and try these."

The house smelled like vanilla the moment I stepped inside. Not the artificial sweetness of a spray but the real, warm scent of a candle burning on the foyer table, a small amber-glass thing with a flame that had been going long enough to fill the hallway. Everything about the entry was intentional in the way Trish seemed to make things intentional — a console table with a small arrangement of dried stems, a coat rack that held things in use, and a mat that had been recently shaken out.

She led me into the yellow kitchen. Thoroughly, committedly yellow. The walls, the dish towels hanging from the oven handle, the ceramic canisters lined up beside the stove, even the checked cushions on the chair seats. It was a kitchen that had decided on a vision and executed it completely. Every available surface held something — a small ceramic rooster, a collection of vintage measuring spoons hung on a strip of wood, stacks of cookbooks with cracked spines and paper markers, a tiered stand of glass spice jars, a hanging calendar from a kitchen supply company still showing

October because nobody had turned it over.

Through the doorway to the living room, I could see the same applied in blue. Different room, different color, same density of objects arranged with the care of a person who found empty surfaces unsettling.

"Nice place," I said, and meant it, because it was. It was a warm house, a house that had been lived in fully, but the accumulation of stuff made me a bit anxious.

"Thank you." She set the tin on the kitchen table next to a wire basket and moved toward the coffee pot. "I've had it fifteen years. I keep thinking I should declutter, and then I look at everything and can't find a thing that shouldn't be there."

I pulled out a chair and sat. My gaze landed on the wire basket. It held a stack of envelopes and loose checks — paper-clipped in clusters, some loose, all of them clearly fundraiser donations based on the kennel club letterhead visible on the remittance stubs tucked between them. A solid stack. More than a few weeks' accumulation. I could see from where I sat that the top check had a date on it, and the date was before Vivian's death.

"You've got a lot of donations to cash," I said.

Trish laughed from the counter, a bright, easy sound. "The club has been blessed this year. People are so generous." She brought two cups to the table, went back for cream and sugar, and settled across from me with the comfortable manner of a woman in her own kitchen, entirely at home. "We've all been so busy since

—" She paused, and the pause did the rest of the sentence's work for it. "Well. You know."

"Vivian," I said.

"Yes." She poured cream into her cup and stirred it slowly. "It's been difficult to stay on top of the administrative things. Normally, she and I would have divided the banking tasks. Now it all falls to me."

"Of course." I added sugar to my coffee and kept my voice even. "How long have those been sitting there?"

"Oh, a couple of weeks, some of them. A few came in just this week." She opened the tin and looked at my cookies with the appraising warmth of a professional baker encountering amateur work and choosing kindness. "These look wonderful, Crystal. Chocolate chip?"

"Yep. My grandmother's recipe." This was true. They were also, I was aware, going to compare unfavorably to anything Trish produced, but I'd made my peace with that before I'd started measuring flour.

She bit into one and made a sound of genuine approval that I chose to believe. "Delicious. Your grandmother knew what she was doing."

We drank our coffee and talked about nothing in particular. The weather, which had turned properly cold overnight, the upcoming regional show, and whether the date would shift given everything that had happened, were all factors in Gerry's efforts to hold the club's morale together by sheer force of administrative will. Trish was easy company. She had the practiced warmth of a woman who had spent years feeding people and making them comfortable, and sitting in her yellow kitchen with good coffee and cookies, it was almost possible to set aside everything else and just be two members of the same club having a Tuesday morning conversation.

Almost.

Trish excused herself to use the bathroom.

I waited until I heard the door close down the hall.

Then I got up and went to the wire basket.

I didn't touch anything. I didn't need to. I stood over the basket and counted what I could see from above — the clusters, the individual checks, the envelopes with remittance stubs visible at the top. I counted twice, quickly, using the paper clips as grouping markers. The clusters ran to six or eight checks each. There were four paper-clipped groups and a loose handful on top. I did the rough math: somewhere between thirty and forty checks, minimum.

I looked at the dates on the ones I could read without moving anything. The oldest I could see clearly was dated three weeks ago. More than a week before Vivian died.

For a club the size of the Riverside Kennel Club, running a fundraiser, a backlog of checks wasn't impossible. But the finance committee treasurer not banking fundraiser income for three-plus weeks, during the lead-up to an audit, was the kind of thing that had an explanation or didn't.

I went back to my seat, picked up my coffee cup, and was looking out the window at the hydrangea bush when Trish came back into the kitchen.

"More coffee?" She was already at the pot.

"Please." I held out my cup. "You must be relieved the audit is almost done."

She poured without pausing. "It'll be good to have it behind us. These things always feel bigger than they are before they're finished." She sat back down and smiled at me across the table. "Clean books, clear conscience. That's what I always say."

I smiled back.

The checks sat in the wire basket between us, three weeks of uncashed donations, and the candle in the foyer burned its vanilla warmth through the house, and I thought about a September ledger that had gone home at the wrong time and an email sent to two people two days before a murder and an audit at the end of the month that was going to look at exactly the kind of accounts where delayed banking created exactly the kind of gaps that a careful person might find very useful.

"Your grandmother's cookies really are excellent," Trish said.

"Thank you," I said. "She was a remarkable woman."

I finished my coffee, thanked her, and left. I needed to do some heavy thinking. The more I knew about

Trish, the more convinced I was that she killed Vivian. All I had to do was prove it.

Chapter Fourteen

The next morning, I worked through my email backlog at the kitchen table with coffee. A tenant inquiry about parking allocation, two invoices from the maintenance crew, and a reminder from the property management software about the quarterly inspection schedule that I'd been moving to next week for three weeks running. I paid the bills that couldn't wait, scheduled the ones that could, and put on my tool belt for a circuit of the building that turned up a loose handrail on the second-floor staircase, a exterior light fixture that had given up entirely rather than just flickering like the laundromat one, and a slow drip from the utility sink in the storage room that I fixed in twenty minutes with a washer replacement and the mild satisfaction that comes from solving a problem with your hands.

By eleven I was done, or done enough, and the dogs had been communicating their position on the morning's priorities with increasing directness. Daisy stationed herself at the door, Minnie spun the circles that meant she'd decided a walk was imminent and simply waited for my participation to become official, and Bella sat in the middle of the kitchen floor staring at me with the unblinking focus she gave when she wanted something and had determined that eye contact was the appropriate tool.

"All right," I said, to no one and everyone. "Let's go."

The halter process took its usual toll. Minnie spun faster once the equipment appeared, which made the actual fitting a moving target. Daisy submitted to hers with the theatrical resignation of a dog enduring something beneath her dignity. Bella made it necessary to retrieve her from the bedroom, where she'd gone the moment she saw me pick up the harnesses, and from there, things proceeded along their usual lines. By the time all three were clipped and leashed, I felt I'd earned the walk as much as they had.

We went the long way down the elm-lined block behind Riverside Towers, through the small park where Bella had once held her ground against a squirrel for forty-five seconds before discretion prevailed, along the river path where the light came through the bare branches in long, flat bars and the ground was soft with recent rain. Daisy found a stick within the first five minutes and carried it the entire route with the pride of a dog transporting something valuable. Minnie trotted with her nose working continuously. Bella walked beside me with the attentive, close-sided gait she adopted on routes she hadn't fully decided were safe, which was most routes.

It was a good walk. The kind that empties the head by filling the senses, that makes the thing you've been turning over for days go quiet long enough to breathe around it. By the time we turned back toward the building, I felt more like myself than I had since the night of the kennel club meeting.

The mail was in when we passed the boxes — Tuesday delivery, reliable as ever. I tucked the stack under my arm and let the dogs lead me back to the apartment, where I unclipped and unharness everyone in the usual reverse chaos, gave out three treats from the jar on the counter, and dropped the mail on the kitchen table while I washed my hands.

Daisy deposited her stick next to the mat by the door, which was where she always put things she intended to retrieve later. Bella went directly to her bed, turned twice, and lay down. Minnie drank from the water bowl with the intensity of a dog who had covered significant ground and knew it.

I sat down at the table and sorted through the stack.

Electric bill. A catalog for garden supplies addressed to the previous property manager, who had moved on three years ago, and whose catalog subscriptions apparently hadn't. A letter from the building's insurance company that would require reading rather than glancing. A reminder from the dentist. Two more bills, one expected and one not. My hand stopped.

The envelope was plain white. Standard size. No return address. My name and the building's address printed in block capitals — deliberate and uniform, the kind of lettering that takes more effort than a quick scrawl.

I looked at it for a moment before I touched it. Just looked at it, sitting among the dentist reminder and the garden catalog, so ordinary in every dimension except the one that wasn't ordinary at all.

My hands trembled as I picked it up. I slid my finger under the flap and opened it. A single slip of paper dropped to the table.

Block capitals again. The same deliberate, effortful uniformity.

STAY OUT OF IT.

Three words. I read them twice, which was unnecessary, and then sat very still in my kitchen chair while Minnie came and put her front paws on my knee and looked at my face with concern.

I put my hand on her head automatically. Then I picked up my phone and called Lance.

He arrived within twenty minutes, which told me he'd been close or had moved fast or both. He came in with his jacket still on and went straight to the table without being directed, taking in the envelope and the slip of paper and their position among the ordinary mail with the attention of a man who had learned not to touch things before looking at them.

"Did you handle the slip?" he asked.

"Just the envelope. The paper fell out when I opened it."

He photographed both where they lay, then bagged them with the kit he kept in his jacket pocket. He sat across from me in the chair that was effectively his at this point and looked at me with the expression that was equal parts concerned and professional. "When did you get the mail?"

"About half an hour ago. We came back from the walk. I brought it up with us."

"You didn't notice anything at the mailboxes? Anyone in the lobby or the common area?"

I thought back. The elm block, the river path, Daisy's stick, the flat afternoon light. Coming back through the side entrance, the mail key, the brief routine of checking the box. "Mrs. Henderson was on her bench. The maintenance van was gone by then. I didn't see anyone near the boxes." I paused. "The mail comes at eleven on Tuesdays. I got back around eleven-thirty. It could have been in there since delivery, or it could have been slipped in after."

"The boxes don't lock properly on the end units," he said. It wasn't a question. He'd noticed this before, in a previous capacity.

"The third one from the left has a latch issue," I confirmed. "It's on my list. Along with approximately forty other things."

He looked at the bag containing the note. "STAY OUT OF IT. Nothing else."

"That was everything."

"Printed, not handwritten. Which means a printer, which means either a home printer or a library or a workplace. Harder to trace, which means whoever sent it thought about that before they sent it." He turned the bag slightly without opening it. "Or they watched enough crime television to know handwriting can be analyzed and adjusted accordingly, which is a different kind of thinking but produces the same result."

"What does it mean that they sent it at all?" I asked. "If someone has killed a person, a note seems like an odd escalation. One is considerably more serious than the other."

"It means they're worried." He set the bag down. "Someone is panicking. They've seen you at the volunteer sessions, at the fundraiser, at Trish's house —" He paused and looked at me.

"She's a suspect," I said. "And she has cookies."

He let that sit without pursuing it. "The point is you've been visible. You were in that restroom. People know you heard something, even if they don't know what. A note is the action of someone who wants you to stop but isn't ready — or willing — to do more than warn."

"Yet," I said.

"Yet," he agreed, and didn't try to soften it.

I got up and poured two cups of coffee, more for the occupation of it than from any particular need for more caffeine, and brought them to the table and sat back down. Bella had migrated from her bed to under my chair, her warmth pressing against my feet. Minnie was back on the sofa. Daisy was asleep beside her stick.

"I keep thinking about the finances," I said. "The note, the timing of it. It came after the email thread. After Gerry said she was going to forward it to you." I wrapped both hands around the cup. "Whoever sent this has something financial to lose. Not reputation, or not only reputation. Something specific and quantifiable that the audit is going to find."

"That's a reasonable assumption.,"

"Trish has uncashed checks sitting in a wire basket on her kitchen table. A three-week backlog, some of which were dated before Vivian died. The September ledger went missing during the exact window between the summer show expenses and Vivian's October presentation to the board." I kept my voice even. "Someone who's been managing accounts in a way that doesn't survive scrutiny would very much want the person scrutinizing them to stop. First Vivian. Now me."

Lance was quiet for a long moment. He drank his coffee and looked at the evidence bag on the table, and did the thing he did when he was thinking through implications rather than information. The slightly inward quality, the stillness.

"The audit firm received Gerry's forwarded email yesterday," he said finally. "They've been in contact with the department. They're expanding the scope."

"To three years? Like Vivian requested?"

"And the show budget line items specifically." He looked at me. "Handler fees. Vendor contracts. Equipment purchases."

Vivian's exact language from the email. The detailed language of a woman who had already identified where to look and needed the professionals to look there too, two days before someone made sure she couldn't follow up.

"When they find something," I said. "And I think they'll find something…what happens to the person who sent this note?"

"If the note connects to the murder, they're looking at considerably more than financial misconduct." He held my gaze. "Which is why I need you to actually stay out of it, Crystal. Not because you're not useful. Because you've become the thing they're most afraid of, and that is not a safe position."

"I didn't do anything to get there," I said. "I was in a bathroom stall."

"And since then, you have done quite a number of things to stay there." His voice wasn't harsh. "The note is a line. I need you to treat it as one."

I looked at the evidence bag. Three words, block capitals, the deliberate effort of someone who'd thought about it before they'd done it. Someone who was frightened enough to warn me but had not, so far, done anything beyond that.

So far.

"All right," I said.

He looked at me steadily. "That was fast."

"I agreed with you," I said. "I do that occasionally."

He reached across the table and put his hand over mine briefly, just a moment, the warmth of it more communicative than anything either of us said. Then he picked up the evidence bag and his coffee and stood.

"Lock the mailbox latch," he said at the door.

"It's on my list," I said.

After he left, I sat at the kitchen table for a while longer, the ordinary mail spread around the space where the envelope had been, the dentist reminder, the garden catalog, and the bills, all of it entirely normal. Bella climbed into my lap from somewhere and settled there with the certainty of a dog who had assessed the situation and determined that this was where she was needed.

I put my chin on top of her head and thought about three words in block capitals and what it meant that someone had taken the time to make them untraceable.

It meant they were careful. It meant they were scared.

And it meant that whatever the audit would find at the end of the month was worth both of those things.

Chapter Fifteen

The next morning, I was on my second cup of coffee and my third attempt at reading the same paragraph of a novel I'd been trying to finish for two weeks when Linda knocked. Not her usual knock. She had a specific rhythm, three quick taps with the knuckle of her index finger. This was two knocks, a pause, then one more, which was the knock of someone who had been moving fast and arrived with something on their mind.

My dogs went into a frenzy of barking which increased when she called out for me to open the door.

I opened the door. She came straight through to the kitchen table and sat down. I put a cup of coffee in front of her before she'd asked because her expression made it clear she needed one.

The dogs investigated her with their standard thoroughness. Minnie pushed her nose against Linda's knee. Daisy sat at her feet and looked up with the patient expectation of a dog waiting for acknowledgment. Bella circled once and returned to her bed, satisfied.

"What happened?" I sat across from her.

She wrapped both hands around the cup. "I was at the dog park this morning. The one on Clement, by the water tower. I go Wednesdays when I have the Henderson's Lab and the Pomeranians from Sycamore Street." She paused. "I got there around eight-thirty. Cold morning, so it was mostly empty. Just me and the three dogs and a woman on the far bench near the fence line."

She stopped.

"Linda."

"It was Trish." She looked at her coffee. "She wasn't there with a dog. She was just...sitting on the bench. Alone. Which is not something you do at a dog park unless you're meeting someone or waiting for someone, but nobody else came and nobody else left and after about ten minutes, I realized she wasn't aware of me at all."

"What was she doing?"

"Crying. Not loudly. Just sitting with her hands in her lap and crying, the way people do when they think nobody's watching. The Henderson's Lab wanted to go toward her, but I redirected him because it felt intrusive, and I'd mostly decided to leave her to it when she started talking."

I set my cup down. "Talking."

"To herself. Or not quite to herself. You know, in

the way people talk when they're working through something and the words are coming out whether they mean them to or not." Linda's hands tightened slightly around her cup. "I wasn't trying to listen. I was at the far end of the enclosure. But it was a quiet morning, and her voice carried."

"What did she say?"

Linda looked at me directly. "She said, *she was going to destroy us.*"

The kitchen was quiet. Outside the window a car moved through the parking lot at the unhurried pace of someone looking for a space, and then that was gone too.

"Those exact words?" I asked.

"Those exact words. Twice. She said it once and then, about thirty seconds later, said it again, quieter, like she was arriving at it rather than repeating it." Linda finally drank her coffee. "Then she wiped her face and sat up straight and looked at the fence for a while, and then she left."

I thought back to the yellow kitchen. The vanilla candle. The wire basket of uncashed checks sitting on the table between us while Trish laughed about how blessed the club had been. The smile that arrived before the explanation. The too-smooth account of the email she hadn't mentioned to anyone.

She was going to destroy us.

Not *me*. Not *the club* or *everything* or any of the other framings a person might use when they spoke about professional consequences or public exposure. *Us.*

"Her family," I said.

Linda nodded slowly. "That's where I landed too."

I thought about what I knew of Trish Donnelly, which was less than I knew of most of the kennel club members because Trish had a quality of being thoroughly present in whatever she was doing — the baking, the committee work, the comfortable warmth of her kitchen — that made it easy to absorb who she was in the room without asking much about who she was outside of it. She talked about the club constantly, about recipes, about the dogs, and about members with the ease of someone for whom community was a natural habitat.

She almost never talked about home.

I'd sat across from her twice now in extended conversation and had come away knowing her flour preferences and her opinion on show venue acoustics and the specific history between Angela and Vivian going back two years. I could not have told you her husband's name until I searched the part of my memory where peripheral details lived and found it there, mentioned once in passing at the Italian restaurant lunch — not by Trish but by Rosemary Dodd, who'd said something about the Donnelly's annual Christmas party being the best-attended event on the street.

"Her husband," I said. "What do you know about him?"

Linda thought for a minute. "Martin. He works in finance. Not locally. I think he consults, works from home mostly. I've seen him at the Christmas show two years running, tall man, quiet, stands slightly apart from things the way people do when they're attending something for someone else's sake." She paused. "Trish mentions him in the way people mention someone who is woven into everything without being visible in any of it. He's there but he's not a subject she brings out, if that makes sense."

It made sense. Some people kept their marriages as the background of their public life, the thing that made everything else possible without ever being the thing they talked about.

"Finance," I said. "He works in finance." He must have been gone or working in a back room when I'd taken the cookies over.

Linda looked at me.

"The club accounts," I said, slowly, following the thread as I said it rather than arriving having already followed it. "Trish chairs the finance committee. She manages the books, the receipts, the banking. But she works in a bakery. Her professional background is in food, in running a small business, in the practical arithmetic of that kind of operation." I turned my cup in my hands. "The reclassification system — the way the show expenses were being categorized, the specific methodology that Vivian objected to and Trish defended. That level of financial architecture, the kind</p>

sophisticated enough that it took Vivian months to document and required an expanded audit scope to properly examine — that's not a baker's instinct."

"You think Martin designed it," Linda said.

"I think Martin may have been more involved in the club's finances than anyone realized." I thought about the uncashed checks in the wire basket. Three weeks of fundraiser donations sitting in a kitchen on a Wednesday morning. Not in a bank account where an audit could track the deposit dates. Not processed through the normal committee protocols. Sitting in a wire basket next to a tin of cookies. "If the money was being moved in ways that benefited someone other than the club, and was sophisticated enough to require professional financial knowledge to construct —"

"Then Vivian wasn't just a threat to Trish's position on the committee," Linda said. "She was a threat to Martin."

She was going to destroy us.

A woman on a bench at eight-thirty in the morning with her hands in her lap, crying in the cold, alone at a dog park with no dog. Not talking about herself. Not talking about her reputation or her committee seat or the years she'd spent building her standing in a club that was, when stripped of everything else, a volunteer organization for people who loved dogs.

Talking about her family. The specific *us* of a marriage. The shared exposure of two people's catastrophe when the life is built together closely enough.

"Linda." I sat forward. "Did she see you?"

"No. I'm certain. She left without looking back and I waited until her car was out of the lot." She paused. "I almost called you from the park but I didn't want to be overheard."

"You did the right thing." I stood and went to the window and looked out at the parking lot without really seeing it. Trish on that corridor on the security footage, six minutes after Angela left. A woman who wasn't visibly distressed, who walked with a purpose she'd covered with the paper towel story. A woman who had known since October that Vivian was building a case. Who had received the email, two days before the meeting, requesting an expanded audit of exactly the line items where the irregularities lived. Who had not mentioned that email to anyone.

Two days to decide what to do. Two days between receiving that email and the night of the meeting.

"She didn't act alone," I said, mostly to hear it outside of my own head. "Or she didn't plan it alone. If Martin was involved in the financial structure, he had as much to lose. More, possibly since he's not a club member. His involvement in the accounts wouldn't be visible unless someone went looking for it. An expanded audit that went back three years and examined every show budget line item and handler fee and vendor contract would find his fingerprints on things that were supposed to only have Trish's."

"Do you think he was there that night?" Linda asked. "At the community center?"

I turned back from the window. "I don't know. Vivian was hit from behind. The voice I heard was controlled, pitched down. I couldn't identify gender from what I heard, just that it wasn't loud and it was deliberate." I thought about this. "But the knife. The premeditation of bringing a knife to a kennel club meeting…that's a level of planning that suggests the decision was made well before arriving. Before the meeting started. Maybe before the day of the meeting."

"Two days before," Linda said quietly. "When the email arrived."

The apartment was very still. Daisy had retrieved her stick from beside the mat and was chewing it with the contentment of a dog with no complicated feelings about the morning. Minnie had climbed onto the sofa and arranged herself in the corner cushion with her chin on the armrest. Bella watched me from her bed with her front paws extended and her dark eyes moving between me and Linda.

"I need to call Lance," I said.

"Yes." Linda nodded. "You do."

"This changes the scope of the investigation. If Martin was involved and if Vivian had documentation that implicated someone outside the club, someone whose professional reputation and livelihood depended on those accounts never being properly examined, then what happened in that restroom wasn't just about protecting a position on a finance committee." I picked up my phone. "It was about protecting a life they'd built together. A business. An income. Everything that goes with a career in financial consulting if it comes out that you've been running a scheme through a volunteer dog club."

Linda was quiet for a moment. Then: "She loves him." She said it without sentiment, just as a fact that mattered. "The way she doesn't talk about him — that's not distance. That's the opposite of distance. Some people keep the things that matter most where nobody can reach them."

I thought about Trish in her yellow kitchen, warm and capable and entirely at home, with her vanilla candle and her wire basket and her too-ready explanations. A woman who had built a careful, comfortable life and had watched it begin to come apart the moment Vivian Cargill started following the money.

She was going to destroy us.

Not anger in those words. Not the hard, bitter quality of someone justifying what they'd done. Just grief, raw and private, on a cold bench at a dog park where nobody was supposed to hear.

Lance answered on the second ring.

"I need to tell you something," I said. "It's about Trish's husband."

Chapter Sixteen

Lance called at six-fifteen the following evening, which was early enough that I was still in the kitchen making something that had started as a real dinner and was trending toward toast. The dogs were in their customary positions for the hour, which meant close enough for me to trip over. Minnie stared with big, sad, dark eyes, Daisy danced on her hind legs, and Bella gave the occasional bark to remind me she was there.

I answered and he said, "Are you home?"

"Yes."

"I'll be there in twenty minutes."

He hung up before I could ask anything, which was either a good sign or a bad sign. I couldn't tell which from two words and a dial tone. I abandoned the dinner project, put bread in the toaster as a contingency, and spent the twenty minutes doing what I always did when I was waiting for something I couldn't hurry. I cleaned the kitchen counter, which didn't need it, and then wiped it again.

He arrived in eighteen minutes, still in his work clothes. He came in, accepted the coffee I already had ready, and sat at the kitchen table with both hands around the cup and the expression of a man organizing what he was about to say.

I sat across from him. Bella immediately positioned herself between our chairs. "Tell me," I said.

"The audit firm finished their preliminary review this afternoon." He turned the cup in his hands once. "Full three-year scope, show budget line items included. Every category Vivian specified in her email."

"What did they find?"

He looked at me steadily. "Eighty-five thousand dollars."

The kitchen went silent. Outside, a car moved through the parking lot and the headlights swept briefly across the window and were gone. I sat with the number and let it settle into the shape of everything that had been building toward it.

"Missing?" I said.

"Gone. Over twenty-six months, beginning approximately two months after Martin Donnelly began informally advising the club on financial recordkeeping." He paused to let that sequence register. "Trish had been treasurer for four years without issue. The irregularities begin at a specific point that coincides directly with Martin's involvement."

"How was it done?"

"Small transfers." He set his cup down. "Nothing large enough to trigger the kind of attention a single substantial withdrawal would attract. The largest single transfer in the entire twenty-six months was four thousand dollars. Most of them ran between eight hundred and two thousand. Some as low as three hundred." He turned the cup again. "Frequent enough to add up. Infrequent enough that the pattern only becomes visible when you look at the full span, which the standard two-year audit scope would have captured the tail of but not the beginning of. The three-year scope caught all of it."

"Which is why Vivian pushed for three years," I said.

"She'd obviously already done the arithmetic herself. The documentation she brought to the October board meeting — the spreadsheets, the receipts she'd tracked — she'd identified approximately sixty thousand of it. She knew the full amount was higher. She knew she needed the professionals to go back further." He looked at me. "She was right about the number. She was right about all of it."

I thought about Vivian Cargill behind her sign-in desk with her clipboard and her too-precise observations about Minnie's weight and ear length. Vivian who collected things like people's vulnerabilities, their secrets, their quiet exposures. Who had walked into a board meeting in October with physical documents laid on the table and a vote request that had split the committee three to two. Who had sent an email two days before she died to the two people with the most power to act on it, one of whom had received it and done nothing, and one of whom had received it and done something that couldn't be undone.

Difficult. Meticulous. Thorough. Every word that had been used about her in my presence now sat differently.

"The transfers," I said. "How were they authorized?"

"Treasurer login credentials. Every single one." Lance's voice was even and careful. He added sugar to his coffee, something I'd never seen him do. "Username and password for the club's financial management system. Every transfer was logged, timestamped, and authorized under Trish's account."

"Could someone else have had her credentials?"

"That's a question the investigation is actively examining." He picked up his coffee, took a sip, grimaced, and set it back down. "There are two possibilities. Either Trish authorized every transfer herself, which places her directly and completely in the center of this. Or someone with access to her login information authorized them on her behalf, which places a second person in the center and Trish in the position of either willing participant or unknowing cover."

"Martin," I said. "Because Linda heard her say that

Vivian was going to ruin 'us'."

He nodded. "Martin Donnelly holds a professional certification in financial management. He has worked independently as a financial consultant for eleven years. His client base is not large . Four regular clients, two of whom we've already spoken with." He paused. "The club accounts represent, by the audit firm's estimate, somewhere between fifteen and twenty percent of the total funds he's managed in the past three years."

"Is any of the eighty-five thousand traceable to him directly?"

"The forensic accounting team is working through it. Small transfers are designed to be difficult to trace by the time they've moved through enough intermediate step." He leaned back slightly in his chair. "What we can establish clearly is the following. The transfers begin when Martin becomes involved. They're authorized under Trish's credentials. They're structured specifically to stay below the threshold that would trigger automatic review flags in the software. And the person who identified them and requested an audit was killed two days after formally notifying the treasurer and the club president of her request."

The sequence laid out like that, in Lance's careful, factual register, was more devastating than any accusation would have been. Not the dramatic language of a crime story but the plain arithmetic of a thing that had happened and been recorded and could now be accounted for.

Eighty-five thousand dollars, moved in increments small enough to hide in the noise of a volunteer organization's ordinary activity. A scheme patient enough to take twenty-six months, careful enough to never take too much at once, sophisticated enough that it had only been found because one meticulous woman had followed the numbers to their source and refused to be redirected.

"She knew," I said. "Trish. She had to have known."

"The investigation hasn't established that definitively."

"Lance." I narrowed my eyes. "She chairs the finance committee. She manages the accounts. She has been managing them for four years. The irregularities begin when her husband becomes involved and the transfers run under her credentials for over two years." I kept my voice level. "She knew. Maybe not the exact figure. Maybe not every transfer. But she knew the shape of it."

He didn't confirm or deny. He was in the careful zone now, the zone where what he could say officially and what he knew privately occupied slightly different spaces. I understood the distinction even when it frustrated me.

"The uncashed checks," I said. "The wire basket on her kitchen table. Three weeks of fundraiser donations sitting there instead of in the bank."

"The audit flagged that too. The deposit timeline

for the fundraiser income is inconsistent with the committee's stated banking protocols." He looked at me directly. "It's consistent with a pattern of delayed processing that creates gaps in the reconciliation timeline."

"Gaps where money can move without the movement being immediately visible," I said.

"That's the working assessment, yes."

I got up, dumped the cup he wouldn't drink, and then poured more coffee for both of us without being asked, because I needed to do something with the particular feeling of a picture coming fully into focus after looking at its pieces for two weeks. I brought the cups back and sat down and Minnie chose this moment to emerge from under the table and arrange herself across my feet with the solid, anchoring weight of a dog who had decided I needed grounding.

"The note," I said. "Stay out of it."

"Printed from a home printer. Standard white paper, standard ink. The kind of printer that exists in approximately forty percent of households and is therefore not usefully specific." He wrapped his hands around the fresh cup. "We can't connect it definitively. Not yet."

"But it came after Gerry forwarded the email to you. After the audit scope was expanded. After the forensic team started looking." I thought about the block capitals, the deliberate uniformity of them, the effort of making them untraceable. "Someone who knew the timeline was closing." Why warn me?" Whoever sent it had to know the police were already involved.

"Someone who was watching the investigation develop and understood what the expanded audit was going to find." He looked at me. "Which means someone who understood the accounts well enough to know what an expanded review would surface. A professional financial consultant would understand that exactly."

Martin. "Where is he now?" I asked. "Martin."

"Home, as far as we know. We haven't moved yet." Lance exhaled heavily. "The forensic accounting review needs another day to finalize the full documentation. We want the complete picture before we move."

"And Trish?"

"Trish is home." A pause. "She went to the dog park this morning. Alone."

I thought about what Linda had described. The empty bench, the cold morning, the words carrying across a quiet enclosure to a woman with three dogs who hadn't been trying to listen. *She was going to destroy us.* The grief in it, the specific register of someone who had already absorbed the worst of it and was sitting with the weight of having let it happen or helped it happen or loved someone who had done it and found herself on the wrong side of the line without ever having meant to cross it.

Or had meant to cross it. That was the question that the investigation was still examining.

"When you move," I said. "Both of them?"

"That's the plan."

Daisy had climbed down from the sofa back and was standing beside Lance's chair looking at him with the expectant patience of a dog who had determined he'd been sitting long enough and should now be paying attention to her. He reached down and scratched behind her ears without looking away from me, the automatic ease of a man who had been coming to this apartment long enough that its dogs were his dogs in the ways that mattered.

"She built a beautiful life," I said, after a moment. The yellow kitchen, the vanilla candle, the knick-knacks on every surface arranged with the care of someone who paid attention to her surroundings. The tin of shortbread and the warm, inclusive smile and the fifteen years in a house she'd made into something. "Whatever she did or didn't know, whatever she did or didn't do…she built something real and she let it become something else."

"Or someone she loved built it into something else," Lance said. "And she chose not to look."

"Is that better or worse?"

He was quiet for a moment. "I don't know. That's not really my part of it."

Outside the window, the parking lot had gone dark and still, the November evening settling in with the flat, definitive quality of a season that had fully committed. Inside the kitchen the light was warm, and the dogs were where they always were, and the coffee was going cool again in the cups.

Eighty-five thousand dollars, moved in increments nobody was supposed to notice, by a woman who may or may not have been watching, on behalf of a man who had understood exactly what he was doing.

And a woman in a restroom who had known all of it and had paid for knowing.

"Lance." He looked at me. "Vivian wasn't easy. She wasn't kind, or at least not often. She made Minnie feel bad about her weight on the first night we met." I rubbed Minnie's side with my foot gently. "But she followed the numbers until she found what was at the end of them. And it cost her everything."

"Yes," he said. "It did."

The toaster on the counter clicked and two slices of bread rose, forgotten and cold, the dinner I'd started and abandoned when the evening had become something else.

Bella put her chin on my knee and looked up at me with her dark, liquid eyes.

I put my hand on her head and left it there as sadness almost overwhelmed me.

Chapter Seventeen

After Lance left, I sat at the kitchen table and didn't move for a long time.

The coffee cups were still there, his and mine, both gone cold. The toaster had given up waiting and the bread had gone stiff in the slots. Outside the window, the parking lot was dark and quiet.

Minnie had reclaimed my feet. Bella was back in her bed but facing me, chin on her front paws. Daisy slept on the sofa with her rubber dachshund toy wedged beside her like a companion.

Eighty-five thousand dollars. Twenty-six months. Transfers small enough to hide in the ordinary noise of a volunteer organization's accounts, large enough, accumulated, to represent a deliberate and sustained theft from people who gave their time and their money to something they loved.

And at the end of it, a woman, dead, on a bathroom floor.

I got up and cleared the cups and the cold toast and wiped the counter and then sat back down, because the cleaning hadn't helped the way I'd hoped. My mind kept returning to the same point, the way it does when there's a piece that won't settle — not the finances, not the methodology, not even the note in block capitals. The restroom. The sequence of it. I'd been turning it over for two weeks and the eighty-five thousand had clarified the motive with a completeness that left only one question still standing, and it was the question that mattered most.

I pulled a notepad from the kitchen drawer, the one I used for maintenance lists and tenant reminders and turned it to a blank page. Not because I needed to write anything down. Because organizing thoughts on paper was a habit I'd had since childhood, since my grandmother had told me that a problem on a page is smaller than a problem in your head because on the page you can see where it ends.

I wrote the sequence the way I knew it, the way I'd known it since the night it happened, refined now by everything that had come after.

Angela and Vivian enter the restroom together at seven forty-three. I know this from the footage. They argue. I heard it, two voices I'd been listening to all evening, carrying through the stall door with the uninhibited volume of a fight that had moved past caring about witnesses. *You can't prove anything. Oh, I can. And I will.*

Not about dogs. Not about ribbons or bloodlines or competition scores. About money. About the eighty-five thousand dollars and the transfers and the three-year audit that Vivian had already set in motion two days prior. Angela didn't know about any of that. Angela's argument with Vivian was the same argument it had always been — the personal, territorial animosity of two women who had been circling each other for two years over a Doberman and a Pomeranian and the question of whose dog deserved to win.

Angela leaves at seven forty-seven. Four minutes, twenty seconds. The footage confirms it. She walks back toward the meeting room at the same pace she arrived, no visible distress. Whatever the argument was, it was the same argument she'd been having for two years, and it ended the same way it always ended — with Vivian still standing and Angela walking away.

Vivian is alive at seven forty-seven.

The restroom is quiet. I'm in the last stall, and I hear the faucet run and the paper towel dispenser and then nothing, and I understand now that the nothing was Vivian alone in the room, perhaps at the mirror, perhaps gathering herself, perhaps sitting with the satisfaction of a woman who had sent her email and initiated her audit and was two days away from a meeting where she planned to say all of it out loud in front of everyone.

She had won. She knew she had won. The question was only how much damage would be done on the way to the finish.

Trish appears on the corridor camera at seven forty-nine.

Two minutes after Angela leaves. I'd asked Lance once whether two minutes was enough time and he'd said it was enough time to confirm the corridor was clear. It was also, I'd thought then and thought more now, enough time to make a decision. To stand on the other side of a door and understand that the window was open and that it would not stay open and that everything depended on what happened in the next few minutes.

She enters the restroom. I hear footsteps — softer than Angela's, lighter, the tread of someone not announcing themselves the way Angela had. Someone who came in quietly. Then the voice I heard but couldn't identify, pitched below the level of recognition, too controlled to be natural. Not a whisper exactly. Something deliberate.

Then the thud.

Here was the question. The one that had been sitting underneath everything else since the night I'd pressed my back against a stall door and counted to ten twice before I could make myself reach for the latch.

The marble soap dispenser lived beside the faucet. Heavy, rounded, the kind of decorative-functional object that community centers buy because it's durable and looks presentable and costs less than it appears to. Blood on the corner of it, specific and directional, the mark of contact rather than splash.

Vivian was struck from behind. Lance had confirmed it from the autopsy without me having to ask. A single blow of significant force, consistent with the dispenser's weight and the angle of the wound. She went down immediately. The knife came after, postmortem, which meant the knife was something else. Staging maybe, insurance, a layer of confusion placed over a scene that already told its own story to anyone looking carefully enough.

Two possibilities. I'd been living with them for two weeks and the eighty-five thousand hadn't resolved them. It had only sharpened the stakes of each.

The first: Trish entered the restroom with the intention of doing exactly what happened. The knife in her bag, brought from home or from somewhere else, evidence of a plan formed in the two days between Vivian's email and the night of the meeting. She knew Vivian would be there. She knew the restroom had been busy and would be busy again and that a window of a few minutes was the most she could expect. She came in, struck from behind, and the dispenser was either the planned instrument, grabbed from the counter in the moment, familiar from whatever reconnoitering she'd done, or incidental, opportunistic, the nearest heavy object at the moment of commitment.

But the knife. The knife complicated the first possibility in a specific way. If the death was planned, you bring the knife and you use the knife. You don't hit someone with a soap dispenser and then use the knife after. You choose one weapon and you use it. The double instrument suggested something less organized than a clean plan. It suggested two different decisions, made at two different moments.

The second possibility was the one that I'd been returning to without wanting to, the one that felt less like a conclusion and more like a door I wasn't sure I wanted to open.

Trish enters the restroom. Vivian is at the mirror or the counter. They argue. The voice I heard, too quiet, Vivian's response inaudible to me but audible in the room. The argument escalates. A push, or a shove, or a stumble. Vivian goes down. The corner of the dispenser.

Accident.

And then panic. The terrible clarity of standing over someone who is not moving and understanding that the choice is no longer about whether something bad has happened but about what you do next. The knife, brought for reasons that made sense two days ago, in the cold arithmetic of a decision made before a meeting about everything that was about to be lost, suddenly repurposed. Not to kill someone who was already dead, but to obscure what had happened. To change the story from a struggle that went wrong to something that looked more deliberate.

A soap dispenser says: someone was here and things got out of hand.

A knife says: someone planned this. Someone with a reason. Someone from outside this room.

I stared at the notepad. The sequence was the same

either way. The outcome was the same. Vivian was on the floor and Trish was in the footage and the eighty-five thousand was gone and the audit was going to find all of it regardless of which version of the restroom was true.

But it mattered. It mattered because Trish on that bench at the dog park, saying *she was going to destroy us* with her hands in her lap and her face unguarded, was not the face of someone who had executed a plan. It was the face of someone living with a consequence they hadn't fully understood they were capable of until it was already done.

I didn't know. That was the honest answer. I didn't know which version of those four or five minutes was the true one, and I wasn't sure the distinction was mine to determine. What I knew was the sequence. What I knew was the motive. What I knew was that a woman who had followed numbers to their source with the patience and precision of someone who believed the truth was worth finding had ended up on a bathroom floor, and that the eighty-five thousand dollars sitting at the center of it had been enough to make someone decide she had to be stopped.

Bella had gotten up from her bed and crossed the kitchen and now sat beside my chair, not asking for anything, not pushing at my hand. Just there. The way she was sometimes, when she'd decided that proximity was the appropriate response to whatever she was reading in the room.

I put my hand down and she pressed the top of her head against my palm and stayed still. I picked her up and tucked her head under my chin. Her warmth soothed me.

Was it an accident. Was it intentional. The question sat in the kitchen with me in the November quiet, and I turned it once more, and understood finally that I had taken it as far as I could take it from where I was sitting.

Lance would find the answer. The forensic accounting would find the money. The investigation would build its case from the outside in, from the evidence to the moment, which was the direction cases traveled when they were built properly.

I had traveled the other direction, from the moment outward, from a locked stall and a thud and three words in block capitals and a wire basket of uncashed checks and a woman crying alone at a dog park at eight-thirty in the morning, and I had arrived at the same place.

Trish Donnelly had been in that restroom.

Whether she had gone in with a plan or left with a consequence, I couldn't say with certainty. But she had gone in. And Vivian had not come out.

I closed the notepad and put it back in the drawer.

Minnie had fallen asleep on my feet sometime while I'd been thinking, her warm weight an anchor. Daisy snored on the sofa. Bella remained warm and soothing in my arms.

I turned off the kitchen light and sat in the dark for

a while and let the question be what it was. Unanswered, important, and no longer mine to carry alone.

Chapter Eighteen

Two days later I stood in the community center doorway with three leashes in my hand and told myself I was only here because Gerry had asked me to come, which was true, and because walking away from an organization in the middle of a murder investigation felt wrong, which was also true, and not at all because I wanted to watch Trish Donnelly's face when she saw me walk in, which was perhaps the truest thing of all and the one I was least proud of. Not to mention that I'd promised to help plan the award's ceremony for the show I'd foolishly entered my dogs in.

The meeting room had the slightly subdued quality of a group that had been through something and hadn't finished processing it — voices a register lower than usual, the social clusters slightly smaller, people standing with their dogs closer to their legs than normal. Colin stood near the window with his jacket on, coffee in hand, and watched the room with the attentive stillness I'd come to associate with him. Angela was absent. Gerry was at the podium end of the room, sorting papers with the organized purposefulness of a woman holding something together by routine.

And Trish was at the refreshment table.

She had her back to the door, setting out a plate of lemon squares with the careful, practiced movements of someone for whom the physical ritual of presentation was automatic enough to perform on autopilot. Her shoulders were set in the way of a person carrying tension they've decided to push through rather than put down. The plate went center table. She adjusted it once, then again, then stepped back.

My three dogs had other ideas.

The leashes went taut without warning, all three at once, and then left my hands entirely. They crossed the room in a flurry of short legs and considerable noise, barking with the conviction of dogs who had detected something their person needed to know about immediately.

Trish gasped and stumbled backward into the table, one hand going to her chest. The plate of lemon squares rocked and settled.

"Control your dogs!" Her voice came out sharp and unsteady, the composure cracked just enough to show what was underneath it.

"I'm sorry." I collected the leashes. Daisy still strained forward, Belle yipped and danced around Trish's ankles, and Minnie still voiced her opinion at full volume. "They aren't usually like this." I looked at

Trish over the top of all three heads. "They must smell something on you."

The pause that followed was brief but complete. Something moved across Trish's face. Not guilt exactly, more the involuntary flinch of a person who has heard a sentence with a second meaning and isn't sure how much of it was intended.

She recovered quickly. The chin came up, and the composure came back down. Her voice found its usual register. "Perhaps Vivian was right to be reluctant about your membership. You and your dogs are a menace."

"Really." I kept my voice mild and gave her the small, unhurried smile I used when I had decided something. "Why don't we step outside? The picnic table out back. I think you and I need to have a conversation." I held her gaze. "I won't take no for an answer."

Her face drained of color. Her gaze flicked to Gerry, who moved toward the podium. I watched her calculate as the meeting was about to start, the public room, the available witnesses, and arrive at the same conclusion I already had.

Outside was better. For both of us.

"Very well," she said.

The picnic table sat on a narrow strip of concrete behind the community center, wedged between the building's rear wall and the beginning of a chain-link fence that bordered the parking lot. A cheerless place designated for those who smoked.

Someone had put a planter of ornamental cabbage beside it that had survived the first frosts and looked defiant about it. The November air nipped my cheeks and still smelled of cold concrete and the distant exhaust of a car running somewhere in the lot.

We sat across from each other. The dogs settled at my feet with the abrupt calm of animals who had made their point and were now prepared to wait. Daisy put her chin on my shoe. Minnie pressed against my ankle. Bella sat upright on the bench seat next to me and watched Trish with the unblinking, forward-eared attention she reserved for things she had decided needed monitoring.

I folded my hands on the table and looked at Trish and tried to find the right entry point into a conversation I'd been mentally rehearsing for two days without managing to get past the opening.

Trish sat with her hands in her lap and looked back. The composure was still there but it was thinner than it had been inside. Out here on a concrete strip in November with nothing between us and the conversation, she was someone else. Smaller somehow, and tired in a way that had been there for a while and was only visible now that she'd stopped performing over it.

I decided the direct approach would be best for both of us. "Trish," I said. "I know about the money."

The hands in her lap tightened. One small, visible movement, quickly stilled.

"I know about the transfers. I know they ran under your credentials for twenty-six months. I know the audit has found approximately eighty-five thousand dollars, and I know the forensic accounting team has been looking at the methodology for several days." I kept my voice even and quiet, not accusatory, just factual. The voice I used when I told a tenant something they needed to know and didn't want to hear. "And I know you were in that corridor on the night Vivian died. The camera put you there six minutes after Angela left. The paper towel story doesn't hold up."

She went very still.

"I'm not the police," I said. "I'm not recording this and I'm not going to repeat it word for word to anyone who isn't Lance. I'm asking you because I think you need to say it to someone before it eats through whatever is left of your soul." I looked at her steadily. "What happened in there?"

The silence lasted long enough that I thought she wasn't going to answer. The ornamental cabbage sat in its planter between us like a small, indifferent witness. In the parking lot a car door closed.

Then Trish's face changed. Not dramatically. There was no sudden collapse, no visible breaking. Just a slow release, like pressure coming out of something that had been holding too much for too long. She looked at her hands in her lap and when she spoke her voice was different from any version of it I'd heard before. Quieter. The warmth now gone, not replaced by coldness but by something more unguarded than either.

"Martin lost our retirement savings." She said it to her hands. "Three years ago. An investment. He was so certain about it, he'd done the analysis, it was going to be the thing that meant we could stop worrying." A pause. "It failed. Not gradually. All at once. Plummeted. We went from being comfortable to being frightened in about six weeks." She stopped. "He didn't tell me for two months. By the time I knew, we'd already borrowed against the house to cover the immediate losses."

I waited.

"The club accounts were right there," she said. "I had access to everything. I'd been treasurer for years and I'd never taken so much as a dollar that wasn't mine. But Martin looked at the structure and said it was possible to. He said we would put it back. That's how he explained it to me. Not taking. Borrowing. From ourselves, almost, because I'd put so many volunteer hours into that club that it owed me something anyway, which is the kind of reasoning that sounds like logic when you're frightened enough." She looked up briefly and then back down. "He set up everything. The small transfers. Below the flag threshold. He said by the time the next audit came around we'd have repaid everything and no one would ever know."

"What happened to the repayment?"

"The investment he was going to use to repay it lost value too." A short, flat sound that wasn't quite a laugh. "So there was another plan. And then another. And the transfers kept going because stopping them would have created a gap that was more visible than continuing, at least that's what Martin said, and I —" She stopped. "I let him keep saying it because I didn't know how to stop and I didn't want to know what happened if we did."

"Until Vivian."

Trish's hands tightened again. "She'd been watching the accounts for almost a year. I knew she was watching. She had this way of asking questions in committee meetings that weren't really questions. She'd ask for clarification on a line item she already understood perfectly, just to see how I answered." She shook her head slightly. "She came to me privately three weeks before the meeting. Before she went to the board, before the email. She came to me first."

"What did she say?"

The pause this time was different this time. Weighted with something specific, something Trish had been carrying with particular difficulty. Her jaw worked once before she found the words.

"She called me a thief in sensible shoes." Trish said it quietly. "She said she'd given me the opportunity to come forward myself and I hadn't taken it, which was true, and that she was done being patient, which I understood, and that she was going to the board and the audit firm and the breed association and that by the time she was finished there wouldn't be a volunteer organization in the county that would accept my participation." She looked at the table. "She wasn't wrong about any of it. That was the worst part. She was completely right and she knew she was right and she wanted me to know she knew."

I let that sit for a moment. Vivian Cargill, behind her sign-in desk with her clipboard, measuring Minnie's weight and ear length with the precision of a woman who believed that accuracy was a virtue regardless of how it felt to the recipient. Vivian in the meeting room, voice carrying above the argument, and Vivian in a private conversation three weeks earlier, delivering a verdict she'd arrived at through months of patient, careful documentation. Difficult. Meticulous. Right.

"And the night of the meeting," I said. "Walk me through it."

Trish looked at the fence line for a long moment, the chain-link and the parking lot beyond it and whatever she saw wasn't any of that. "I saw her go toward the restroom. I'd been watching her all evening because I knew she was going to make her announcement at the banquet and I didn't —" She stopped. Restarted. "I didn't have a plan. I want you to understand that. I didn't go in there to do anything. I went in because I needed to try one more time. To ask her to let us repay it quietly, to give us until the end of the year, to please not do this in public at the banquet in front of everyone." She paused. "Martin was terrified after her email. He said she'd implied she had evidence that would end his consulting career entirely, not just with the club. He wanted me to have the knife for protection. He was frightened." Her voice caught on the last word and then steadied. "I was frightened."

"You went in after Angela left."

"I waited in the hallway. I heard Angela come out and I counted. I don't know why I counted, I just stood there and counted to sixty and then went in." She shook her head faintly. "Sixty seconds. As if that made it less of a decision."

"What was Vivian doing when you came in?"

"Standing at the mirror. She heard me come in and looked at my reflection and her expression —" Trish paused. "She wasn't surprised. She looked like someone who had been expecting a conversation and found it slightly beneath her schedule. She said, *Trish. I wondered how long you'd wait.* Just like that."

I could hear it. The clipped precision of a woman who had anticipated the approach and prepared her response before the door opened.

"What did you say?"

"I asked her to wait. To give us more time. I told her about Martin's investment, about the retirement savings, about the plan to repay it — the whole thing, standing in a community center restroom, which is not where I imagined having that conversation when I rehearsed it." A brief, painful sound. "She listened. She let me finish. And then she said —" Trish stopped.

"What did she say?"

"She said that what I had just described was not a repayment plan, it was a confession, and that she intended to use it as one." Trish's voice had gone very flat. "She said some people spend their whole lives in sensible shoes without ever understanding that sensible and decent weren't the same thing. That she'd watched me for a year move club money to cover a grown man's mistakes and call it borrowing. That the word I was looking for was stealing." She looked at her hands. "Then she turned back to the mirror."

The dismissal of it. The deliberate, precise turning away, as if the conversation was finished because Vivian had decided it was finished. I understood, sitting on that concrete bench in the November cold, the specific quality of rage that gesture could produce in someone who had come with everything exposed — the retirement savings, the borrowed house, the fear, the years of small transfers — and been handed back a word and a turned back.

"I grabbed her arm," Trish said. "I didn't think about it. I grabbed her arm and she pulled away and she was closer to the counter than I realized…she lost her balance and…" She stopped.

The parking lot was silent. Even the dogs were still, Bella's ears fully forward, reading something in the quality of the air.

"She went down," Trish said. "The corner of the counter caught her head. The soap dispenser." A pause so long I almost spoke into it. "The sound. I will never

—" She stopped again. Her hands were white at the knuckles. "I went down on my knees beside her. I didn't know what to do. I put my hand on her shoulder, and I called her name. She didn't answer. I thought —" Her voice fractured for the first time, a single clean break, quickly repaired. "I thought she was dead."

I waited.

"I put my fingers on her neck." Trish said it very quietly. "The way you're supposed to. The side of the neck." She demonstrated the motion with her own hand, two fingers against her own throat, and then lowered it back to her lap. "She had a pulse. She was breathing. I could feel it and I could see it. Her chest was moving, just slightly, but moving."

The cold air sat between us.

"Trish." My voice came out careful and very even. "She was alive."

"Yes." The word was barely audible.

"And you walked away."

The silence that followed was different from every silence before it in the conversation. Not the silence of someone organizing their thoughts or steadying their voice. The silence of someone who had arrived at the center of the thing they'd been moving toward and found it exactly as terrible as they'd known it would be.

"Yes," she said again.

I sat with that. The restroom sequence that I'd been reconstructing for two weeks rearranged itself around this single fact. A piece that had been missing had now been found. Not a push and an impact and a death. A push and an impact and a woman on the floor with a pulse, and another woman making a decision.

"You put the knife there," I said.

"I was on the floor beside her, and she was breathing and I told myself she would be fine." Trish's voice had the specific quality of someone reciting a thing they had said to themselves many times in the dark. "That she would come around and someone would find her and she would be fine. That I could leave and it would be an accident and nobody would need to know I was there." She paused. "I told myself that while I took the knife out of my bag."

"While she was still breathing."

"While she was still breathing." A long pause. "I didn't use it to — I want to be precise about this. I placed stuck it in a non-lethal place on her…I didn't —" She stopped. "She was already on the floor. I told myself it would look like someone else had done it, someone who had come in after me, someone with a real reason. Angela. Or someone we didn't know. I told myself a lot of things in those two or three minutes."

"And then you left."

"And then I left." She said it with the flat, unvarnished precision of someone who had stopped finding ways to soften it. "I went back to the meeting room, and I sat down and Colin was saying something about the show schedule, and I looked at my hands and they were shaking and I put them in my lap and waited." She paused. "I told myself she would be found quickly. That she would be fine. That the pulse I felt was strong enough to pull through a non-lethal stabbing."

"But you didn't go get help," I said. "You didn't open the door and call for someone. You didn't pull the fire alarm or find Gerry or do any of the things you could have done while she was still breathing."

The words weren't an accusation. They were just the shape of it, laid out plain.

"No," Trish said. "I didn't."

I understood, sitting across from her in the cold, what the distinction meant in the eyes of the law and beyond it. A push in a heated moment was one thing — terrible, consequential, but shaped by passion and proximity and the specific combustion of two people in a small room with a year of pressure between them. What came after was something else. A pulse felt and acknowledged. A decision made in full knowledge of what she was leaving behind. The knife stuck into a woman who still breathed as a misdirection, a deliberate rewriting of the scene, while the woman herself moved from alive toward not alive on a bathroom floor.

That was the line. Not the push. The leaving.

"She was going to destroy everything," Trish said again. "The house. Martin's career. Everything we'd built. She was going to stand up at that banquet and say it all in public and there would have been nothing left."

"And instead," I said, "she died on a bathroom floor while you sat in a meeting about the show schedule."

Trish closed her eyes briefly. When she opened them, the exhaustion was total, every layer of the composed, capable, warm-kitchened woman she presented to the world worn through to something much simpler and much heavier underneath.

"Yes," she said. "Instead, she died."

We sat in the quiet. A gust of wind moved through the parking lot and rattled the chain-link fence and passed. Bella had moved at some point during the conversation from her watchful seat to lean against Trish's leg, the small warm weight of her pressed against an ankle that belonged to someone whose life was about to become unrecognizable. Trish looked down at her and the composure that had held through everything finally gave way.

She put her hand on Bella's head. "She really is perfect," she said. Her voice was entirely different now. Small. "Vivian was right about that. She was right about a great many things."

"She was," I said.

The lemon squares were still inside on the table. The meeting still went on behind the building's wall, Gerry's voice carried faintly through the brick. A room full of people who had known Vivian and not liked her and had stood around her body and not been surprised, had gone home to their dogs and their ordinary lives while the woman responsible had sat among them for two weeks, bringing shortbread and refilling coffee cups and overexplaining routine audits with the energy of someone managing a fire they could feel through the floor.

"You need to go to Lance today," I said. "Not tomorrow. Today, before the meeting ends and before you go home and think of reasons not to." I kept my voice quiet and without cruelty. "Tell him what you told me. The retirement savings, Martin's involvement, what happened in that restroom. All of it, including the part about the pulse."

She nodded. A small, certain motion, the nod of someone who had already arrived at this conclusion before I said it and had been waiting for the permission of having it said out loud.

"The pulse," I said, because it needed to be named one more time. "Trish. Whatever else happens — whatever the law makes of the push, whatever Martin's involvement means for his part in it — the pulse is what it is. You felt it and you knew and you made a choice. That's the thing you have to say."

"I know." She looked at her hands. "I've known since I walked back into that meeting room. I knew the moment I sat down." A pause. "I've known every morning since. I know it the same way every day. It doesn't get smaller."

"No," I said. "I don't imagine it does."

Bella pressed harder against her leg, the

uncomplicated warmth of a small animal offering what small animals offer. Not understanding, not absolution, just presence. Trish kept her hand on Bella's head and looked at the fence line and breathed the cold air and I gave her another minute because a minute seemed like the least that was owed.

Then I stood and gathered the leashes and Bella peeled away from Trish's leg and returned to my side with the gentle obedience she saved for moments when she sensed I needed her close.

"I'm going to go find Gerry," I said. "I'll tell her you need a few minutes before you come back in. That's all I'll say."

Trish nodded.

"And then I'm going to call Lance."

She nodded again.

I looked at her one more time — at the apron she still wore from the refreshment table, at the cold-reddened hands in her lap, at the tiredness in her face that had been there for two weeks and was now, somehow, slightly different in quality. Not lighter. But more honestly carried. The exhaustion of someone who has put down a performance rather than a weight.

"The lemon squares are very good," I said, because I didn't know what else to say and it was true.

Something moved across her face. Not a smile. Closer to the memory of one. "My mother's recipe," she said.

I left her at the picnic table in the November cold

and took my three dogs back through the community center's rear door, past the bulletin board and the corridor and the restroom with its handwritten Out of Order sign that someone kept replacing and went to find Gerry.

Behind me the chain-link fence rattled once more in the wind and went still. The dog show tomorrow and the award ceremony after would be a lot different than years past.

Chapter Nineteen

The banquet hall was the community center's largest room, opened up for the occasion with the folding partition walls pushed back to reveal the full space that existed behind the meeting room on ordinary Tuesdays. Someone had made a genuine effort with the decorations. Round tables draped in white with small floral centerpieces that featured dogs worked into the arrangements in a way that managed to be charming rather than absurd. Ribbon displays ran the length of the far wall, blue, red, and yellow, the accumulated wins from a year's worth of competitions arranged by category, with the pride of an organization that took its achievements seriously. A small podium stood at the front with the club's banner behind it, and the lighting was warm enough that the whole room had the quality of an event that wanted to feel significant and had put in the work to get there.

I stood in the doorway with three dachshunds and took a moment to look at it before going in.

Gerry was already at the front, speaking with Colin, who had his professional composure fully assembled for the evening and was wearing a dark jacket. He caught my eye briefly and nodded once. Whatever they were discussing was quiet and purposeful and I didn't try to read it from across the room.

Angela was there. I hadn't been certain she would be, and the fact of her presence, alone, at a table near the ribbon wall, Sweetie Pie sitting at her feet with the show-ring composure of a dog who understood formal occasions, said something about her that I respected. She had every reason to stay home. She'd been taken in for questioning, her name had moved through this club's gossip circuit for weeks, and the murder had attached itself to her publicly in ways that were going to take time to detach. She was there anyway, back straight, coffee in front of her, wearing the expression of a woman who had decided that the room belonged to her as much as anyone else and intended to occupy it accordingly.

Rosemary Dodd sat at a center table with the Bichon on her lap and Carol Fenton beside her. They'd been kind to me in the way of people who weren't sure what to say but wanted to say something. I appreciated it more than I'd told them.

Colin had separated from Gerry and was making a slow circuit of the room with the professional eye of someone checking sight lines and arrangements. He paused near the ribbon display, straightened one that had shifted slightly, and moved on.

Trish was not there.

The space where she would normally have been, the refreshment table, was empty. Someone had put out store-bought cookies in a clear plastic tray. Nobody had touched them.

I hadn't told anyone what had happened at the picnic table except Lance. I'd called him the moment I was back inside, and the conversation had been brief and specific, ending with him saying he'd handle it. What that meant in terms of timing I hadn't known until this morning, when he'd texted two words — *tonight, probably* — and I'd read it standing in my kitchen with a halter in my hand and Bella already retreating down the hall.

Which was why I was in my best dress at a kennel club banquet with a feeling in my chest that had nothing to do with the occasion and everything to do with knowing what was coming and not knowing exactly when.

I knelt in front of my three in the doorway, eye level with six small dark eyes, and said, "You three had better behave better than you did during the show."

The show had been…an experience. Minnie had woofed at every dog we passed on the circuit. Daisy's coat had staged a full rebellion sometime between the grooming table and the ring, the smooth surface I'd spent forty minutes brushing into submission chose that moment of public presentation to develop opinions of its own, sticking up in directions that suggested creative interpretation rather than breed standard. And Bella had looked at the ring, assessed its requirements, and determined that walking was not something she was prepared to offer on this occasion, leaving me to carry her through the entire circuit while she surveyed the audience with the dignified composure of a dog being transported rather than shown.

It had not been a competitive outing. Colin had watched from the side of the ring with an expression of careful neutrality that I suspected concealed a significant amount of amusement.

Maybe I should hire him to train them. I dismissed the thought immediately. I wasn't renewing my membership. The Riverside Kennel Club had given me one murder, two suspects, a financial fraud, an anonymous threatening note, and a woman's confession on a cold concrete bench, and I had been a member for less than a month. The math did not favor renewal.

Bella gave a sharp, indignant yip at my tone.

"Don't," I said. "You know exactly what you did."

Daisy and Minnie stared at me with the wide-eyed innocence of dogs who had decided that stillness and eye contact constituted a complete defense.

I stood up, took the leashes, and went to find Linda.

She had claimed a table toward the middle of the

room, not the back, where I would have chosen, but not the front either. A reasonable compromise. She had already had a glass of wine and wore something dark blue that made her look composed, elegant, and entirely at ease with herself.

"You clean up nice," she said, as I pulled out my chair.

"Thanks. I own three dresses." I looped the leashes around the chair leg and sat. "The choice took longer than it had any right to."

"The green suits you." She looked at the dogs, who arranged themselves under the table with the resigned competence of animals accepting an indoor situation. "How did the show go?"

"We have a future in abstract expressionism," I said. "Traditional show ring, less so."

She laughed quietly and refilled her glass, and I looked around the room one more time and thought about the feeling in my chest and named it, finally, for what it was.

It wasn't anticipation. It wasn't satisfaction. It was a heaviness that comes from knowing that something is about to happen that cannot be undone, and that is necessary and that will hurt people regardless of whether they deserve it, and sitting in a decorated room waiting for it to arrive.

Gerry took the podium at seven-thirty with the warm, carrying voice of a woman who had been running meetings for years and understood that the difference between a speech and a conversation was mostly about not losing the room in the first thirty seconds.

She thanked the members. She thanked Colin for his work on the show. She thanked Trish for — she paused at the name, a fraction of a beat, invisible to most people in the room — for her years of service to the club's administrative work. She said it with the care of someone placing something fragile down gently and moved forward.

She talked about the year. The competitions, the community work, and the fundraiser that had exceeded its goal. She talked about difficulty, not naming it but naming its shape. The loss, the uncertainty, the ways in which a community is tested by what happens within it, and is made by how it responds.

Then she picked up the card for the People's Choice award.

People's Choice was voted on by the membership at the show itself. Not a judge's decision, not a breed standard calculation, just the collective preference of the people in the room for the dog that had made them feel something during the day. It was the least official ribbon and, Gerry had told me once in passing, usually the most meaningful.

"This year's People's Choice award," Gerry said, and looked down at the card, and looked up with an expression of genuine pleasure that was the most unguarded thing I'd seen from her in weeks, "goes to

Minnie Waters."

I blinked.

Linda made a sound beside me. Not quite a laugh, more the sound of something she'd been expecting that had arrived exactly on time.

From under the table came a single, resonant woof, as if Minnie had heard her name and confirmed her availability.

I reached down and unlooped her leash, and she emerged from under the table with the unhurried dignity of a dog who had never doubted this outcome. The room laughed, warmly, genuinely, the first fully unguarded sound I'd heard from the group in weeks. Minnie walked with me to the podium and accepted the ribbon from Gerry's hands with the composure of someone receiving something long overdue. Gerry crouched and scratched her ears, and Minnie permitted it with regal restraint.

"She woofed at every dog in the ring," I said quietly to Gerry.

"That's why they voted for her," Gerry said. "She had opinions. People appreciate that." She stood and squeezed my hand briefly, and in the squeeze was something more than congratulations. Acknowledgment, maybe, of the picnic table and the phone call and the thing that was still coming. "Thank you, Crystal," she said, quietly enough that the room couldn't hear. "For all of it."

I took Minnie back to our table. She climbed into

my lap, ribbon still attached to her collar and sat there with the authority of a dog who had made her point.

"People's Choice," Linda said.

"Don't," I said.

She smiled into her wine.

Lance came through the door at seven fifty-three.

He was in his jacket with his badge visible, which was the thing that changed the room before anything else happened. Not his face, which was professionally neutral, not his pace, which was measured, but the badge, catching the warm banquet lighting and registering in the peripheral vision of the people nearest the door, spreading outward in a ripple of redirected attention.

He had two officers with him. I recognized one. Neither of them looked at me, except for one long, lingering gaze as Lance glanced at my dress with approval. I might have to wear one more often.

The room had gone quiet by the time he reached the center. A collective stilling, ears rotating, several animals pressing closer to their humans.

Angela looked at Lance and then looked at me, and something in her expression said that she had already arrived at the right conclusion and simply waited for it to become official. She sat very straight in her chair.

Lance crossed the room to the table where Martin Donnelly sat.

Martin. Quiet Martin, who stood slightly apart at

events and attended for Trish's sake. He'd come tonight in a dark jacket, hair combed, the presentable composure of a man doing what was expected of him, and he'd been sitting with the stillness that I now understood differently than I had when I'd first catalogued it. Not the stillness of a quiet man at his wife's social occasion. The stillness of a man waiting, the way Trish had been waiting.

He stood when Lance reached him. A small thing, that standing — voluntary, without resistance, the movement of a man who had made the calculation and arrived at his answer before anyone spoke.

Lance said something quietly. Martin nodded once. The officers moved.

The murmur moved through the room in a wave.

"Trish?" someone said, from a table near the back, the name carrying the specific weight of a question that already knew its answer.

Lance met my eyes once across the room as he moved Martin toward the door. Not a long look. Just acknowledgment, and something underneath it that I understood as the acknowledgment of what acknowledgment couldn't hold — the picnic table, the pulse, the twenty-six months of small transfers, and the woman who had felt a heartbeat and chosen silence.

Trish had turned herself in that afternoon. Lance had told me in a text at four-thirty: *She came in. Thank you.* Two sentences. The door closed behind Lance, the officers, and Martin Donnelly.

Angela Merritt set her coffee cup down on its saucer with a small, precise sound and looked at the ribbon wall for a long moment. Then she looked at the room. At Gerry behind the podium, at Rosemary and Carol at their center table, and at Colin standing very still near the door through which Lance had just left.

"I assume," she said, in the clear, carrying voice of a woman who had been waiting two weeks for the right moment and understood that this was it, "that my name can now be removed from whatever unofficial list people have been keeping."

It wasn't a question.

Gerry looked at her from behind the podium "Angela, on behalf of this club, I am sorry. For the suspicion and for the weeks that followed and for what was done to Vivian and what was taken from all of us." She looked at the room. "This club has not been what it should have been. I think most of us have known that for longer than Vivian's death made it undeniable." A pause. "That changes. Starting now, with transparency, with proper governance, and with the understanding that no single person should ever again have unchecked access to accounts that belong to everyone in this room." She set down her notecards. "That is my commitment to you. If you'll have me in this role to honor it."

The room remained quiet.

Then Rosemary Dodd began to clap, a little tentatively, and Carol Fenton joined, and it spread from there. Not thunderous, not the applause of an occasion, but the genuine, collective response of people who had been waiting for something to be named and had heard it named correctly at last.

Angela didn't clap. She picked up her coffee cup and inclined her head toward Gerry in the smallest possible nod of acknowledgment, which, from Angela, I had come to understand was the equivalent of a standing ovation.

I sat at my table with Minnie in my lap and the People's Choice ribbon against my hand and Linda beside me. The room continued around me in its complicated, damaged, resilient way.

It wasn't triumphant. That was the thing that surprised me, though it shouldn't have. I'd felt it building since the picnic table, since Trish's hands in her lap, and the quiet devastation of *yes, she was breathing*. Victory was the wrong shape for an evening that had ended with a man in handcuffs and a woman somewhere in a room with a lawyer, describing a pulse she'd felt and a choice she'd made.

What it was, was over. Or the beginning of over. The heaviness that comes after something has been resolved that never should have needed resolving, that started with a woman nobody liked very much doing the right thing meticulously and paying for it completely.

Minnie shifted in my lap and looked up at me with her dark, steady eyes and the People's Choice ribbon swung against my wrist.

"You deserved it," I told her.

She woofed once, quietly, as if she'd never had any doubt.

Chapter Twenty

Three weeks after the banquet, I sat at my kitchen table with a cup of coffee. The morning light came through the window at the low, flat angle of December, the kind of light that makes ordinary things look considered, and I sat in it and did nothing in particular for a few minutes, which was something I was relearning how to do.

Bella slept on the sofa. Daisy had her stick — a new one, sourced from the park on Tuesday's walk, already awarded the permanent indoor status she granted all sticks she considered exceptional. Minnie pressed against my ankle under the table, warm and snoring, her People's Choice ribbon hanging from the hook by the door where I'd put it the night of the banquet and hadn't moved it since. Not as a trophy exactly. More as a reminder of something I hadn't fully named yet.

The Riverside Kennel Club had held an emergency board meeting the week after the banquet. Gerry had presented a governance reform proposal that ran to eleven pages, which I knew because she'd emailed it to the full membership with a cover note that was three sentences long and characteristically direct. New financial oversight protocols. Dual authorization is required for any transfer above $500. An independent treasurer rotating every two years, elected by membership vote rather than appointed by the board. The vote to adopt it had been unanimous, which Linda told me afterward was the first unanimous vote the board had taken on anything in four years.

Colin Hart had offered, quietly and without announcement, to waive his handler's fee for the next show season and put the amount toward the repayment fund the club had established for the members whose donations had been among the transferred funds. He hadn't made a speech about it. Gerry had told me over coffee, and I'd thought about the letters in the filing cabinet and the account discrepancy from two years ago and said nothing, because some debts get paid in ways that don't require an audience.

Angela had won three ribbons at the regional show the following weekend. I knew this because Linda sent me a photograph. Sweetie Pie mid-gait, head perfectly level, Angela at the other end of the lead with the expression of a woman entirely at peace with the distance between herself and everyone else in the ring. I'd looked at it for a long time before putting my phone down.

Vivian's sister had come from out of state to handle the estate. Linda had met her briefly at the club when she came to collect Vivian's personal items from the office. A small woman, Linda said, with her sister's precise way of holding herself but none of her sharpness, who had accepted the condolences offered with the quiet dignity of someone who had loved a difficult person and was not interested in revising the love now that the difficulty was confirmed. She'd taken the Pomeranians, Honey and Sugar, home with her. I was glad about that. They were good dogs.

Martin Donnelly had been charged with fraud, embezzlement, and conspiracy. His lawyer had entered a not guilty plea that nobody, as far as I could tell, expected to survive contact with eighty-five thousand dollars of forensic accounting documentation. Lance said very little about the case specifics, which was normal, but he said it like someone who considered the outcome reasonably certain and was focused on making sure the process was airtight rather than fast.

Trish had been charged with second degree murder.

I'd looked up the distinction after Lance explained it — the difference between the first and second degree, the legal weight of the word *intent,* and how it was applied to a sequence of events in which the killing blow was arguably unplanned but the choice that followed it was not. Second degree captured something that the first degree wouldn't have, and manslaughter didn't quite reach. A death that began in a moment and was completed in a decision.

She had pleaded guilty.

I'd heard this from Lance on a Wednesday evening, sitting at this same table with coffee that had gone cold in the usual way, and I'd sat with it for a long time after he told me. Not with satisfaction, not with grief exactly, but with the specific weight of something that was both correct and costly in a way that the law could account for and nothing else quite could.

The vanilla candle probably sat, not burning now, in her foyer. The yellow kitchen was probably still yellow. Fifteen years of a house made into a home, and the home was still there, and Trish was not in it. Nor was her husband.

I thought about her hand on Bella's head at the picnic table. The way she'd said *she really is perfect* with the composure finally gone and nothing underneath it but the plain truth of a woman who had loved dogs and baked well and made increasingly terrible decisions out of love for a man who had asked too much of her and let her carry it.

I didn't know what to do with that. I suspected I wasn't supposed to know, that it was the kind of thing that sat in you permanently rather than resolving, and that sitting in it without resolution was its own kind of reckoning.

Linda knocked at eight-thirty with her customary three-tap rhythm, which restored something in my chest that I hadn't noticed had been slightly off-register.

She came in, assessed the kitchen, checking that everything was where she expected it, and poured herself a coffee with the ease of someone entirely at home.

"How are you?" she asked.

"Good." I meant it. "Genuinely."

She nodded. "Good."

She sat across from me, and we drank our coffee. Daisy emerged from the sofa to investigate whether Linda had brought anything interesting, found she hadn't, and retired back to her stick.

"Gerry called me yesterday," Linda said. "She wants to talk to you about taking a more formal role with the club. Administrative something. She said, and I quote — she needs someone with practical experience, a level head, and no investment in the existing politics."

"She said that about me?"

"She said it about the role. I inferred the rest." Linda's expression was serene. "You'd be good at it."

"I'm not renewing my membership," I said. "I said that at the banquet."

"You said it before the banquet, too." She picked up her cup. "And before the volunteer morning. And before the Italian restaurant." She looked at me. "At some point, the pattern becomes the answer."

I looked at the People's Choice ribbon on the hook by the door. At Minnie who still pressed against my ankle. At the window, the December light was streaming in at a low angle.

The washing machine in the laundromat was running properly. Mrs. Henderson's kitchen sink had been resolved. The parking lot light had been replaced and budgeted for the following year. Riverside Towers was in reasonable order, which meant the days would have their ordinary shape again — bills and tenant emails and the minor, manageable crises of a building full of people living their lives.

It was enough. It was more than enough. It was exactly the life I'd chosen and continued to choose every time I had the option to choose differently.

"Tell Gerry I'll think about it," I said.

Linda smiled into her coffee like someone who had already known that was the answer.

Lance came for dinner that evening. He brought wine and the information, delivered without ceremony while I was making pasta, that the forensic accounting team had officially closed their review and submitted their final report. The number had come in at eighty-seven thousand, four hundred and twenty dollars. The two thousand difference from the preliminary estimate was a handful of smaller transfers that had been harder to trace through the intermediate steps, but had ultimately led back to the same place everything else led.

"Is it strange," I asked, stirring the sauce, "that I know the exact amount?"

"No," he said. "It's strange that you got involved in the first place."

"I was in a bathroom stall."

"You were in a bathroom stall," he agreed. He sat at the table, poured the wine, and watched me cook with the easy, comfortable attention of someone who was exactly where he wanted to be.

Minnie sat under his chair. Daisy lay on the sofa with her stick. Bella did her end-of-evening circuit of the apartment, checking each room, satisfying herself that everything was as it should be before settling for the night.

She came back into the kitchen and sat down beside my feet and looked up at me with her dark, liquid eyes that saw more than I could account for and communicated it in ways that required no translation.

"All clear?" I asked her.

She blinked once, slowly, and went to her bed.

I served the pasta and sat across from Lance. We ate dinner in the warm December kitchen of a building I managed, and an apartment I'd made into a home. Outside, the parking lot lights came on at their usual time, and somewhere on the second floor, Mr. Pacheco's television murmured through the wall, and the ordinary world resumed its ordinary turning.

Minnie started to snore under Lance's chair.

The People's Choice ribbon hung by the door.

And in the morning, there would be emails to answer and light bulbs to check and a laundromat that occasionally required attention, and three dachshunds who would need walking in the cold December air with their halters that none of them particularly wanted, and a life that was quiet and useful and entirely mine.

It was, I thought, more than enough.

It was, in fact, exactly right.

www.cynthiahickey.com
Cynthia Hickey is a multi-published and best-selling author of cozy mysteries and romantic suspense/thrillers. She has taught writing at many conferences and small writing retreats. She and her husband run the publishing press, Winged Publications. They live in Arizona and Arkansas, becoming snowbirds with three dogs. They have ten grandchildren who keep them busy and tell everyone they know that "Nana is a writer."

Connect with me on FaceBook
Twitter
Sign up for my newsletter and receive a free short story
www.cynthiahickey.com

Follow me on Amazon
And Bookbub
Shop my bookstore on my website for better prices and autographed books.

Enjoy other books by Cynthia Hickey

COZY MYSTERIES

Daring Dachshund Mysteries
Off the Leash
A Killer in the Kennel Club

The Tail Waggin' Mysteries
Cat-Eyed Witness
The Dog Who Found a Body
Troublesome Twosome
Four-Legged Suspect
Unwanted Christmas Guest
Wedding Day Cat Burglar
The entire Tail Waggin' Series

Tiny House Mysteries
No Small Caper
Caper Goes Missing
Caper Finds a Clue
Caper's Dark Adventure
A Strange Game for Caper
Caper Steals Christmas
Caper Finds a Treasure
Tiny House Mysteries boxed set

A Hollywood Murder
Killer Pose, book 1

Killer Snapshot, book 2
Shoot to Kill, book 3
Kodak Kill Shot, book 4
To Snap a Killer
Hollywood Murder Mysteries

Shady Acres Mysteries
Beware the Orchids
Path to Nowhere
Poison Foliage
Poinsettia Madness
Deadly Greenhouse Gases
Vine Entrapment
Shady Acres Boxed Set

Nosy Neighbor Series
Anything For A Mystery
A Killer Plot
Skin Care Can Be Murder
Death By Baking
Jogging Is Bad For Your Health
Poison Bubbles
A Good Party Can Kill You

Romantic Suspense and Thrillers

The Sheriff of Misty Hollow
Girls' Weekend Survival
The Threat

Evil Returns
Drowned in Silence
Banner of Death
Christmas Burns
High Stakes
The Alphabet Murders
He's Coming For You

Cowboys of Misty Hollow
Cowboy Jeopardy
Cowboy Peril
Cowboy Hazard
Cowgirl Blaze
Cowboy Uncertainty
Cowboy Christmas Crisis
Cowboy Pitfall
Snowed in For Christmas With a Cowboy

Stay on the Ranch with the whole set

Misty Hollow
Secrets of Misty Hollow
Deceptive Peace
Calm Surface
Lightning Never Strikes Twice
Lethal Inheritance
Bitter Isolation
Say I Don't
Christmas Stalker
Bridge to Safety

When Night Falls
A Place to Hide
Mountain Refuge
Silent Retribution

Stay in Misty Hollow for a while. Get the entire series here!

Secrets of the South
The Lovers' Lane Murders
The Prom Night Hitchhiker
Up in Smoke

The Seven Deadly Sins series
Deadly Pride
Deadly Covet
Deadly Lust
Deadly Glutton
Deadly Envy
Deadly Sloth
Deadly Anger
Get the whole set here

Brothers Steele
Sharp as Steele
Carved in Steele
Forged in Steele
Brothers Steele (All three in one)

The Brothers of Copper Pass

Wyatt's Warrant
Dirk's Defense
Stetson's Secret
Houston's Hope
Dallas's Dare
Seth's Sacrifice
Malcolm's Misunderstanding
The Brothers of Copper Pass Boxed Set

Highland Springs

Murder Live
Say Bye to Mommy
To Breathe Again
Highland Springs Murders (all 3 in one)

Colors of Evil Series

Shades of Crimson
Coral Shadows
Indigo Nightmares
Read the whole set!

The Pretty Must Die Series

Ripped in Red, book 1
Pierced in Pink, book 2
Wounded in White, book 3
Worthy, The Complete Story

Lisa Paxton Mystery Series

Eenie Meenie Miny Mo
Jack Be Nimble
Hickory Dickory Dock
Boxed Set

Hearts of Courage
A Heart of Valor
The Game
Suspicious Minds
After the Storm
Local Betrayal
Hearts of Courage Boxed Set

Overcoming Evil series
Mistaken Assassin
Captured Innocence
Mountain of Fear
Exposure at Sea
A Secret to Die for
Collision Course
Romantic Suspense of 5 books in 1

Wife for Hire – Private Investigators
Saving Sarah
Lesson for Lacey
Mission for Meghan
Long Way for Lainie
Aimed at Amy

Wife for Hire (all five in one)

One Hour (A short story thriller)
One Night (a short story thriller)
One Day
One (the set)

Nosy Neighbor collection

Christmas with Stormi Nelson

The Summer Meadows Series
Fudge-Laced Felonies
Candy-Coated Secrets
Chocolate-Covered Crime
Maui Macadamia Madness
All four novels in one collection

The River Valley Mystery Series
Deadly Neighbors
Advance Notice
The Librarian's Last Chapter
All three novels in one collection

Cozies not part of a series
Coffee, Tea, or Murder
Scones to Die For
Mischief and Mayhem

Time Travel

The Portal

Historical cozy
Hazel's Quest

Historical Romances
Novellas
Runaway Sue
Taming the Sheriff
Sweet Apple Blossom
A Doctor's Agreement
A Lady Maid's Honor
A Touch of Sugar
Love Over Par
Heart of the Emerald
A Sketch of Gold
Her Lonely Heart
Abigail's Proposal
Sophia's Hope
Moira's Quest
Savannah's Trial
Josephine's Dream
A Most Reluctant Bride
Competing Hearts
A Teacher's Heart
Lesson of Love

SERIES
Finding Love the Harvey Girl Way
Cooking With Love
Guiding With Love
Serving With Love
Warring With Love
All 4 in 1

Finding Love in Disaster
The Rancher's Dilemma
The Teacher's Rescue
The Soldier's Redemption

Woman of courage Series

A Love For Delicious
Ruth's Redemption
Charity's Gold Rush
Mountain Redemption
They Call Her Mrs. Sheriff
Woman of Courage series

Short Story Westerns
Flowers of the Desert

Contemporary

Romance in Paradise
Maui Magic

Sunset Kisses
Deep Sea Love
3 in 1

The Red Hat's Club (Contemporary novellas)

Finally
Suddenly
Surprisingly
The Red Hat's Club 3 – in 1

STANDALONES
Finding a Way Home
Service of Love
Hillbilly Cinderella
Unraveling Love
I'd Rather Kiss My Horse

Whisper Sweet Nothings (a Valentine short romance)

Christmas Romances (Contemporary and Historical)
Dear Jillian
Romancing the Fabulous Cooper Brothers
Handcarved Christmas
The Payback Bride
Curtain Calls and Christmas Wishes
Christmas Gold
A Christmas Stamp

Snowflake Kisses
Merry's Secret Santa
Holly's Hope
A Christmas Deception
A Christmas Castle

Heads up! Some of the links above are affiliate links. If you decide to buy through them, I may earn a small commission (thank you for supporting my work!). It doesn't change the price for you.